"Rather than saying the author is influe
we say that the author enables Nietzsch
innovate, and enrich themselves?"

    —Farid Younes

Spoiled, cocky, pompous . . . and irrepressibly witty, Farid Younes organizes his script for dramatic effect.

    —Dr Mohammad El Hajj, Architecture, Lebanese University

You are a dangerous man, Farid.

    —Michel Aoun, President of Lebanon

The author has an intense approach to challenging Friedrich Nietzsche, one of the greatest minds that ever lived . . . brilliance, amusement, and satisfaction for the soul.

    —Dr Robert Haddad, University of Notre Dame, Lebanon
    Author of *Elias Michel Haddad, Un pionnier de la*
    caricature au Liban entre 1942-1962

If Nietzsche wakes up and reads this book by Farid Younes, we should quickly duck for cover.

    —Dr Paul Jahshan, University of Notre Dame, Lebanon
    Author of *Cybermapping and the Writing of Myth*

Memories do not tease us, they just tease themselves! And that is the genuinely special nature of *Nietzsche Awakens!*

    —Habib Younes, Lebanese University
    Author of *Cloud and Dust Icons*

When you stimulate a dead person to answer, he inhabits your mind forever.

    —Dr Ameen Albert Rihani, past Vice-President,
    University of Notre Dame, Lebanon
    Author of *Multiculturalism and Arab American Literature*

To be a philosopher is to be inhuman. Radiance in the form of a book.

> —Dr Desirée Sakkal, Lebanese University
> Author of *Modernism Movement* and *Researches in Philosophy between Avicena and Plato*

If we cannot contradict the belief of the so called "past," then the earth ceases to turn. Is it an Eternal Recurrence? These questions start popping up every time you finish a chapter of *Nietzsche Awakens!*

> —Father Dr Elie Keserwany, Paris IV Sorbonne, University of Notre Dame, Lebanon

NIETZSCHE aWAKENS!

MATCHING WITS WITH FRIEDRICH

FARID YOUNES

Cune

Nietzsche Awakens!
Matching Wits with Friedrich
by Farid Younes
© 2022 Farid Younes
Cune Press, Seattle 2022
First Edition

Paperback ISBN 9781951082017
EPUB ISBN 9781614574132

Library of Congress Cataloging-in-Publication Data

Names: Younes, Farid, author.
Title: Nietzsche awakens! : matching wits with Friedrich / Farid Younes.
Description: Seattle : Cune Press, 2022.

Nietzsche Awakens! is a philosophical work, written entirely in aphorisms. It is an analytical way to trigger readers to think:

The first part of *Nietzsche Awakens!* consists of "modifying" Nietzsche's aphorisms, either to contradict his sayings, or to be even more cynical than he is, or to explore new dimensions to his thinking. The second part consists of persuading Nietzsche to accept the author's refutation.

Rather than being influenced by Nietzsche, the author is bringing Nietzsche alive. Rather than saying the author is influenced by Nietzsche, can't we say that the author enables Nietzsche's aphorisms to expand, innovate, and enrich themselves?

Identifiers: LCCN 2019037751 | ISBN 9781951082017 (paperback) | ISBN 9781614572190 (kindle edition) | ISBN 9781614572206 (ebook) | ISBN 9781614572213 (ebook other)
Subjects: LCSH: Nietzsche, Friedrich Wilhelm, 1844-1900. | Nietzsche, Friedrich Wilhelm, 1844-1900--Quotations. | Aphorisms and apothegms.
Classification: LCC B3317 .Y48 2019 | DDC 193--dc23
LC record available at https://lccn.loc.gov/2019037751

Bridge Between the Cultures (a series from Cune Press)

Jinwar and Other Stories	Alex Poppe
Empower a Refugee	Patricia Martin Holt
The Dusk Visitor	Musa Al-Halool
Afghanistan & Beyond	Linda Sartor
Stories My Father Told Me	Helen and Elia Zughaib
Kivu	Frederic Hunter
White Carnations	Musa Rahum Abbas
The Passionate Spies	John Harte
Music Has No Boundaries	Rafique Gangat

《》Cune   Cune Press: www.cunepress.com | www.cunepress.net

Contents

Introduction

WHY DO WE READ THE great philosophers? Their thinking shapes our world and imbues our lives with subtle tones that give us our sense of what it means to be alive, to be free, to hope, to love. The great philosophers have provided us with a mental fabric that allows us to express humanity and to regard ourselves as civilized.

And yet the words of the great philosophers, and their lives, often seem archaic or irrelevant to modern concerns. This book is my dialogue with one of these philosophers, a thinker who has helped me pull my life together and who gives me hope that I can become a better person in the years to come.

Friedrich Nietzsche, the "bad boy" of Western Thought, was born in 1844 in Germany and died in 1900. He came along rather late in the game. Plato, for example, had a significant head start. What's more, Nietzsche suffered from poor health. He was ignored, if not scorned, by the intellectual and cultural leaders of his day. And his unpublished work was curated by his sister who bent it to support the growing German nationalism that followed World War I—thereby tainting his work as "fascist" or "Nazi" . . . which was a poison kiss for a cultural figure following World War II. By the 1960s, however, corrected editions of his writings became available and his writing was cited by Jean-Paul Sartre and others. Some credit him as a source of the skeptical movement called Existentialism that became popular as a sober assessment of life against the triumphalism of capitalism and democracy as conceived by Western leaders and their national business interests in the late 1950s.

Today, Nietzsche is well worn and no longer at the hot center of campus rage against the capitalist machine. He is, simply, passé. In the current pool of ignorance and neglect of all things intellectual and of Nietzsche in particular, we find the space to discover this man trough his words. His ideas are accessible and are especially powerful when imbibed in sips, a few sentences at a time.

Playing tag with Friedrich Nietzsche is amusement, sport, an exercise to keep one's mind alive. In Part One of this book, I present my own rephrasing of some of Nietzsche's most well known aphorisms. Then, in Part Two, I invite Nietzsche to refine and reformulate my own aphorisms. Since Nietzsche is not with us today . . . this means that I am inviting the reader to supply the great philosopher's responses.

What I am trying to do is to concretize "The Eternal Recurrence" which Nietzsche defines in his *Notebooks* as ". . . a circular movement of absolutely identical series . . . ." The Eternal Recurrence proves ". . . that the world as a cycle has already repeated itself infinitely often and plays its game *ad infinitum.*"

If we dialogue with Nietzsche and other great minds of the past, it can be a way of using their intelligence and wisdom to spark our own response: our imagination, insight, and understanding of who we are and who we can become.

I live in the coastal city of Byblos in northern Lebanon. I have a family, practice architecture, and teach philosophy and cultural studies in the local university. On weekends and holidays I retire to think and write in the Lebanese mountains. From my simple cabin I can walk to a point where I can see down the steep slopes with their mountainside villages to the distant urban fringe below, then the water's edge and beyond an ancient sea, the Mediterranean.

I live a peaceful and meditative life. I enjoy my work as a designer and I delight in my students. Yet, like all of us in Lebanon, I have been immersed for nearly a decade with scenes of horrific cruelty from nearby Syria and unbearably desperate refugees here in Lebanon. In the deeper past we had the Lebanese civil war, and for the last couple of years we have had a financial breakdown of the national economy and the Lebanese government—also there was a "really big" explosion in Beirut.

In this modern world of violence and suffering where barbarism is in the air we breathe, playing gentle games with Friedrich Nietzsche can be a way of restoring one's soul and placing a bet that ultimately the guns will fall silent, the raging tirades of the world's dictators and buffoons will fade, and humanity will be restored, one thoughtful word at a time.

Farid Younes
Byblos, Lebanon
January, 2022

Editor's Note:
Uncredited text is by the author, Farid Younes.
In "Beginning" and similar chapters, the bulleted text is by Farid Younes.

Beginning

"I know my fate. One day my name will be associated with the memory of something tremendous—a crisis without equal on earth, the most profound collision of conscience, a decision that was conjured up *against* everything that had been believed, demanded, hallowed so far. I am no man, I am dynamite."
Ecce Homo[1]

- I know my fate. Soon my name will replace the memory of your name of something tremendous—a crisis without equal on earth, the most profound collision of conscience, a decision that was conjured up against everything that had been believed, demanded, hallowed so far. "I am no dynamite, I am *Human, All Too Human.*"

"I stay to mine own house confined,
Nor graft my wits on alien stock:
And mock at every master mind
That never at itself could mock."
The Joyful Wisdom[2]

- I stay to mine own house confined,
grafting your wits on alien stock, Friedrich
And mock at every master mind
That never at itself could mock.

"By means of it, I do honor to a thing, I distinguish a thing; whether I associate my name with that of an institution or a person, by being against or for either, is all the same to me."
Ecce Homo[3]

- By means of it, I do honor to a thing, I distinguish a thing; whether I associate my name with you Friedrich, by being *against* or *for* either, is all the same to me.

"My time has not yet come either; some are born posthumously."
Ecce Homo[4]

- My time has already come; some are born famously.

"Posthumous people (me, for instance) are understood worse than contemporary ones but *heard* better. More precisely: no one ever understands us – and *that's* what gives us our authority. . . "
The Twilight of the Idols[5]

- Posthumous people (you, Friedrich, for instance) are understood worse than contemporary ones but *heard* better. More precisely: I understood you perfectly—and that's what gives you misery. . .

"No shepherd, and one herd! Everyone want the same; everyone is equal: he who hath other sentiments goeth voluntarily into the madhouse."
Thus Spake Zarathustra[6]

- No shepherd, and one herd! Everyone wanteth the same; everyone is equal: he who hath other sentiments goeth voluntarily into the madhouse: I am in your home, Friedrich.

"Oh Zarathustra, your fruits are ripe but you are not ripe for your fruits!"
Thus Spoke Zarathustra[7]

- Oh Nietzsche, your fruits are ripe but you are not ripe for my fruits!

"I will never again read an author of whom one can suspect that he *wanted* to make a book, but only those writers whose thoughts unexpectedly became a book."

Human, All Too Human[8]

• I will never again read an author of whom one can suspect that he wanted to make a book, but this one only were my thoughts unexpectedly became this book.

"Lured by my style and tendency.
you follow and come after me?
Follow your own self faithfully—
Take time–and thus you follow me."

The Gay Science[9]

• Lured by your style and tendancy, Friedrich ?
you follow and come after me?
Cure your own self faithfully—
Take time—and thus you follow me.

"Imitators. A : 'What ? You don't want to have imitators?'
B: 'I don't want people to do anything after me ; I want everyone to do something before himself (as a pattern to himself) just as I do.'
A: 'Consequently?'"

The Joyful Wisdom[10]

• Imitators. A : "What ? You don't want to have imitators?"
B: "I don't want people to do anything after me; I want everyone to do something before himself (as a pattern to himself) just as I do."
A: Here it is.

I

FRIEDRICH, YOUR RECURRENT THOUGHTS ARE NOT ETERNAL!

1
On Contradictions

"**Not that you lied to me, but that I no longer believe you, has shaken me.**"
Beyond Good and Evil[1]

- Not that you lied to me, but that I no longer believe myself, has shaken me.

"**With a great goal. With a great goal one is superior even to justice, not only to one's deeds and judges.**"
The Gay Science[2]

- With a great goal. With a great justice one is superior even to his goal, not only to one's deeds and judges.

"**What? You are looking for something? You want to multiply yourself by ten, by a hundred? You are looking for disciples? Look for *zeros*!**"
The Twilight of the Idols[3]

- What? You are looking for something? You want to multiply yourself by ten, by a hundred? You are looking for disciples? Remove the zeros!

"**. . . decide slowly and tenaciously hold on to what has been decided. Everything else follows.**"
Nietzsche's Last Notebooks 1888[4]

- . . . decide slowly and tenaciously hold on to what has not been decided. Everything else follows.

"**Poor. He is now poor, but not because everything has been taken from him, but because he has thrown everything away:—what does he care ? He is accustomed to find new things—It is the poor who misunderstand his voluntary poverty.**"
The Joyful Wisdom[5]

- Poor. He is now poor, but not because everything has been taken from him, but because he has thrown, willingly, everything away:—what does he care? He is accustomed to beg—It is the rich who understand easily his foolish poverty.

"**It is not the victory of science that distinguishes our nineteenth century, but the victory of scientific method over science.**"
Writing from the Late Notebooks[6]

- It is not the victory of science that distinguishes our twentieth one century, but the failure of the scientific method in science.

"**. . . for everything that has a price has little value.**"
Thus Spoke Zarathustra[7]

- . . . for everything that has a price has no value.

"**The fundamental fact of 'inner experience' is that the cause is imagined after the effect has taken place.**"
Writing from the Late Notebooks[8]

- The fundamental fact of "inner experience" is that the cause takes place after the effect has taken place.

"**When we are awake we also do in our dreams: we invent and make up the person with whom we associate—and immediately forget it.**"
Beyond Good and Evil[9]

- When we are awake we also do in our dreams: we imagine and make up the person with whom we associate—and he will never forget it.

"Indeed, whoever possesses little is possesses all the less: praised be a small poverty!"
 Thus Spoke Zarathustra[10]

- Indeed, whoever is in no need to possess possesses all the less: praised be a small poverty!

"It is invisible hands that torment and bend us the worst."
 Thus Spoke Zarathustra[11]

- It is too visible hands that torment and bend us the worst.

". . . but whoever obeys, he does not hear himself!"
 Thus Spoke Zarathustra[12]

- . . . but whoever obeys, he does willingly hear himself!

"What strange, wicked, questionable questions!"
 Beyond Good and Evil[13]

- What strange, wicked, answerable questions!

"The pain (Schmerz or <agony>) is something other than the desire—I want to say, it is not the opposite."
 Nietzsche's Last Notebooks 1888[14]

- The pain is the same as the desire—I want to say, it is not the opposite.

"What is the difference between believers and remains one deceived? No one lied when he is well."
  Nietzsche's Last Notebooks 1888[15]

- What is the difference between believers and remains one deceived? Nothing if he was badly mistaken.

"Concerning Eloquence. What has hitherto had the most convincing eloquence? The rolling of the drum: and as long as kings have this at their command, they will always be the best orators and popular leaders."
  The Joyful Wisdom[16]

- Concerning Eloquence. What has hitherto had the most popular eloquence? The rolling of the drum: and as long as kings have this at their command, they will always be the best orators and convincing leaders.

". . . but lacked the music in the womb."
  Nietzsche's Last Notebooks 1888[17]

- . . . but lacked the womb in the music.

"Spirit and character. Some reach their peak as character, but his spirit is not up to this height, while with others it happens the other way around."
  The Gay Science[18]

- Spirit and character. None reach their peak as character, because his spirit is not accustomed to this height, while with others it occurs the other way around.

"The belief in truth begins with the doubt of all truths in which one has previously believed."
  Human, All Too Human[19]

- The belief in truth begins with the belief of all "truths" in which one has previously believed.

"The first discoverer is usually that quite ordinary and unintellectual visionary—chance."
Human, All Too Human[20]

- The first discoverer is usually that quite brilliant and intellectual fantasist—chance.

"Praise in Choice. The artist chooses his subjects; that is his mode of praising."
The Joyful Wisdom[21]

- Concealments in Choice—The artist chooses his subjects; that is his mode of cheating.

"Most people are much too much occupied with themselves to be wicked."
Human, All Too Human[22]

- Most people are much too much wicked to be occupied with themselves.

"Always at Home. One day we attain our *goal*—and then refer with pride to the long journeys we have made to reach it. In truth, we did not notice that we traveled. We got into the habit of thinking that we were at home in every place."
The Joyful Wisdom[23]

- Always elsewhere. Never will we attain our *goal*—and then refer with pride to the long journeys we have made to reach it. In truth, we did not notice that we travelled. We got into the habit of thinking that we were elsewhere in every place.

"You do not love your knowledge enough anymore, as soon as you communicate it."
Beyond Good and Evil[24]

- You adore your knowledge, as soon as you communicate it/with it.

". . . there is no 'being' behind doing, acting, becoming. 'The doer' is merely a fictitious addition to the doing; the 'doing' is all."
Genealogy of Morals[25]

- . . . there is no "doing", nor acting, neither becoming behind being. "The actions" are merely fictitious additions to the being; the "being" is all.

"Wood and cliff know worthily how to keep silent with you."
Thus Spoke Zarathustra[26]

- Wood and cliff know worthily how to exchange with you.

". . . no honey is sweeter than that of knowledge. . ."
Human, All Too Human[27]

- . . . no bitterness is sweeter than that of knowledge. . .

"The culture of a people as the opposite of that barbarism has been defined, appropriately, I think, as unity of artistic style in all the vital manifestations of a people."
Unmodern Observations[28]

- The culture of a people as the opposite of that barbarism has been defined, appropriately, I think, as unity of values in all the vital manifestations of a people.

"The flame is not as bright to itself as it is to those it illumines: so too the sage."
Human, All Too Human[29]

- The flame is not as bright to itself as it is to those it illumines: so too the fool.

"Another century of readers and spirit itself will stink."
Thus Spake Zarathustra[30]

- Another century of authors and spirit itself will stink.

"But that is not the danger of the noble one, to become a good one, but to become an insolent, a sneering one, a destroyer."
Thus Spake Zarathustra[31]

- But that is not the danger of the noble one, to become a good one, but to become nobler.

"Mystical explanations are regarded as profound; the truth is that they do not even go the length of being superficial."
The Joyful Wisdom[32]

- The scientific positivist explanations are regarded as profound; the truth is that they do not even go the length of being superficial.

"We get on with our bad conscience more easily than with our bad reputation."
The Joyful Wisdom[33]

- We get on with our bad reputation more easily than with our good conscience.

"Well, there actually are things to be said in favor of the exception, *provided that it never wants to become the rule.***"**
  The Gay Science[34]

- Well, there actually are things to be said in favor of the rule, *provided that it never wants to become the exception.*

"*What do you love in others?***—My hopes."**
  The Gay Science[35]

- *What do you love in others?*—My despairs.

"Even God has his hell: it is his love for mankind."
  Thus Spoke Zarathustra[36]

- Even man has his hell: it is his love for God.

"We must understand how to obscure ourselves in order to get rid of the gnat-swarms of pestering admirers."
  Human, All Too Human[37]

- We must understand how to expose ourselves in order to let the gnat-swarms of pestering admirers escape.

**"The crabs are, with whom I have no sympathy,
you attack it, it taverns [traverses];
can you hear them, it works backwards."**
  Nietzsche's Last Notebooks 1888[38]

- The crabs are, with whom I have no sympathy,
  you attack it, it taverns;
  you release, it pinches.

"If you don't want your eyes and mind to fade,
Pursue the sun while walking in the shade."
The Gay Science[39]

- If you don't want your eyes and mind to fade,
  Pursue the shade while walking under the sun.

"Impoliteness is often the sign of a clumsy modesty, which when taken by
surprise loses its head and would fain hide the fact by means of rudeness."
Human, All Too Human[40]

- Arrogance is often the sign of a clumsy modesty, which when
  taken by surprise loses its head and would fain hide the fact by
  means of rudeness.

"Worst, however, are petty thoughts. Indeed, better to do evil than to
think small!"
Thus Spoke Zarathustra[41]

- Worst, however, are generous thoughts. Indeed, it is further evil to
  think generously!

"We become hostile to many an artist or writer, not because we notice in
the end that he has duped us, but because he did not find more subtle
means necessary to entrap us."
Human, All Too Human[42]

- We become hostile to many an artist or writer, not because we
  notice in the end that he has duped us, but because he did not find
  more subtle means necessary to entrap himself.

"What dost thou think most humane?—To spare a person shame."
The Joyful Wisdom[43]

- What dost thou think most humane?—To stimulate a person's shame.

"Machinery is impersonal; it robs the piece of work of its pride, of the individual merits and defects that cling to all work that is not machine-made—in otherwords, of its bit of humanity."
Human, All Too Human[44]

- The person is a machine; it robs the piece of work of its pride, of the individual merits and defects that cling to all work that is not machine-made—in otherwords, of its bit of machinery.

"When we have first found ourselves, we must understand how from time to time to lose ourselves and then to find ourselves again—This is true on the assumption that we are thinkers. A thinker finds it a drawback always to be tied to one person."
Human, All Too Human[45]

- When we have first discovered ourselves, we must understand how from time to time to deconstruct ourselves and then to reconstruct ourselves again—This is true on the assumption that we are thinkers. A thinker finds it a drawback always to be limited to one person.

"Faith means not *wanting* to know the truth."
The Anti-Christ[46]

- Reason means not *wanting* to know the truth.

"A true fox not only calls sour the grapes he cannot reach, but also those he has reached and snatched from the grasp of others."
Human, All Too Human[47]

- A true fox not only calls sour the grapes he cannot reach, but also those he will reach and snatch from the grasp of others.

"'One is not discourteous when one knocks at a door with a stone when the bell-pull is awaiting'—so think all beggars and necessitous persons, but no one thinks they are in the right."
  The Joyful Wisdom[48]

- "One is not discourteous when one knocks at a door with a stone when the bell-pull is awaiting"—so think all donors and affluent persons, but no one thinks they are in the right.

". . . The boredom of God on the seventh day of Creation would be a subject for a great poet."
  Human, All Too Human[49]

- . . . The boredom of God before the seventh day of Creation would be a subject for a great poet.

"However great be my greed of knowledge, I cannot appropriate aught of things but what already belongs to me—the property of others still remains in the things. How is it possible for a man to be a thief or a robber?"
  The Joyful Wisdom[50]

- However great be my greed of knowledge, I cannot yield aught of things but what already belongs to me—the property of others still remains in the things. How is it possible for a man to be a feeder or a benefactor?

"The best author will be he who is ashamed to become a writer."
  Human, All Too Human[51]

- The best author will be he who is ashamed to become an author.

"Only when he has attained a final knowledge of all things will man have come to know himself. For things are only the boundaries of man."
Daybreak[52]

- Only when he has attained a final knowledge of himself will man have come to know all things. For man is only the boundaries of things.

"Those who seek wit do not possess it."
Human, All Too Human[53]

- Those who have but wit still seek wit.

"In Applause. In applause there is always some kind of noise: even in self-applause."
The Joyful Wisdom[54]

- In Applause. In applause there is always some kind of silence: even in self-applause.

"You've got back into the crowd:
the crowd will be smooth and hard.
The loneliness wearing down [*mürbt*]…
spoil the solitude. . ."
Nietzsche's Last Notebooks 1888[55]

- You've not got back into the crowd:
  the crowd will be smooth and soft.
  The loneliness uses, rots and spoils any crowd. . .

"What is the Seal of Attained Liberty?—To be no longer ashamed of oneself."
The Joyful Wisdom[56]

- What is the Seal of Attained Liberty?—To be no longer ashamed of the *raison d'être* of one existence.

**"Your false love
to the bygone,
a gravedigger love—
it's a predator alive
they steal it from the future."**
Nietzsche's Last Notebooks 1888[57]

- Your false love
  to the bygone,
  a gravedigger love—
  it's a predator alive
  they steal the future from a bygone.

"I could believe only in a God who would know how to dance."
Thus Spake Zarathustra[58]

- I could believe only in a God who would know how to humanize.

"Without Vanity—When we love we want our defects to remain concealed—not out of vanity, but lest the person loved should suffer therefrom. Indeed, the lover would like to appear as a God, and not out of vanity either."
The Joyful Wisdom[59]

- Honestly—When we love we want our defects to remain shown—it is only by honesty to lest the person loved should suffer therefrom. Indeed, the lover would like to appear as a God, and this, too, honestly.

"You hold it any longer,
thy imperious fate?
Love it, it you have no choice!"
　　　Nietzsche's Last Notebooks 1888[60]

- You hold it any longer,
  thy imperious fate?
  let it love you, it he has no choice!

"To become wise we must *will* to undergo certain experiences, and
accordingly leap into their jaws. This, it is true, is very dangerous. Many
a 'sage' has been eaten up in the process."
　　　Human, All Too Human[61]

- To become wise we must *will* to undergo certain experiences, and
  accordingly leap into their jaws. This, it is true, is very peaceful.
  Many a "sage" has eaten even the process.

"I alter too quickly: my to-day refuteth my yesterday. I frequently overleap
steps when I ascend no step pardoneth me for that."
　　　Thus Spake Zarathustra[62]

- I alter too quickly : my to-day refuteth my yesterday. I frequently
  beat the steps when I ascend, all steps pardoneth me for that.

"Throw your heavy deep!
People forget! People forget!
A divine (Göttlich) art of oblivion!
Want to fly
will you be home at heights:
throw your heaviest in the sea!
Here is the sea, cast into the sea!
A divine art of oblivion!"
　　　Nietzsche's Last Notebooks 1888[63]

- Carry your heavy deep!
  People remember! People remember!
  A divine [Göttlich] art of remembering!
  Want to fly
  Will you be home at heights:
  carry the sea with your heaviest!
  Here is you, cast the sea into you!
  A divine art of remembering!

"'Will to Truth'—that might be a concealed Will to Death."
  The Joyful Wisdom[64]

- Will to Death"—that might be a concealed Will to Truth.

"If the essence of Being [*Wesen des Seins*] is will to power. . ."
  Nietzsche's Last Notebooks 1888[65]

- If the power of Being (Wesen des Seins) is will to be the Essence. . .

"To our strongest drive, the tyrant in us, not only our reason bows but also our conscience."
  *Beyond Good and Evil*66

- To our strongest drive, the tyrant in us, not only our reason bows but also our heart.

"But I ask impossibilities. I ask my pride to be always the companion of my wisdom. And when once my wisdom leaveth me: alas! It liketh to fly away! Would that my pride would then fly with my folly!"
  Thus Spake Zarathustra[67]

- But I ask impossibilities. I ask my pride to be always the companion of my wisdom. And when once my wisdom leaveth me: alas! It liketh to fly away! Would that my pride would then stay with my me!

"Love, too, has to be learned."
The Gay Science[68]

● To learn, too, has to be loved.

". . . how from the beginning we have contrived to retain our ignorance in order to enjoy an almost inconceivable freedom, lack of scruple and caution, heartiness, and gaiety of life - in order to enjoy life!"
Beyond Good and Evil[69]

● . . . how from the beginning we have contrived to retain our ignorance in order to enjoy an almost inconceivable dependence, lack of scruple and caution, heartiness, and gaiety of life - in order to enjoy life!

"Every habit makes our hand more witty and our wit less handy."
The Gay Science[70]

● Every habit makes our hand more clumsy and our clumsiness wittier.

"Most thinkers write badly because they communicate to us not only their thoughts but also the thinking of their thoughts."
Human, All Too Human[71]

● Most thinkers write badly because they communicate to us not only their thoughts but also what they are not thinking of their thoughts.

"When virtue has slept, it will arise more vigorous."
Human, All Too Human[72]

● When vice has slept, it will arise more vigorous.

". . . we have art so that we go not to the underlying truth."
Nietzsche's Last Notebooks 1888[73]

- . . . we have truth so that we go not to the underlying art.

"A scholar of old things . . .
a gravedigger and crafts,
a life of coffins and sawdust"
Nietzsche's Last Notebooks 1888[74]

- A scholar of new things . . .
  a gravedigger and crafts,
  a life of coffins and sawdust.

"The wittiest authors evoke the least perceptible smile."
Human, All Too Human[75]

- The wittiest authors evoke the least imperceptible teardrop.

2
On Cynicism

"Too long he sat in a cage,
Run away this!
he feared a too long
Jailers:
He is now fearful of its path:
Everything makes him stumble,
the shadow of a stick already makes him stumble"
Nietzsche's Last Notebooks 1888[1]

- Too long he sat in a cage,
  Run away this!
  he feared a too long
  Jailers:
  He is now fearful that jailers, of its path:
  Everything makes him stumble,
  the shadow of his stick already makes him stumble

"Before one we look for man, we must have found the lantern—Will it
have to be the Cynic's lantern?"
Human, All Too Human[2]

- Before one we look for truth we must have found the man—Will
  it have to be the Cynical man?

"The great wars of the present age are the effects of the study of history."
Daybreak[3]

- The great wars of the present age are the effects of the study of civic
  education.

"Many a peacock hides his tail from every eye—and calls it his pride."
Beyond Good and Evil[4]

- Many a peacock hides his tail from every eye—and calls it his chastity.

"The philanthropy of the sage sometimes makes him decide to pretend to be excited, enraged, or delighted, so that he may not hurt his surroundings by the coldness and rationality of his true nature."
Human, All Too Human[5]

- The Hypocrisy of a "friend" sometimes makes him decide to pretend to be excited, enraged, or delighted, so that he may not hurt his surroundings by the coldness and rationality of his true nature.

"O my brothers, am I then cruel? But I say: that which is falling should also be pushed!"
Thus Spoke Zarathustra[6]

- O my brothers, am I then cruel? But I say: that which is falling I should do nothing, only watched and enjoyed!

"One does not attack a person merely to hurt and conquer him, but perhaps merely to become conscious of one's own strength."
Human, All Too Human[7]

- One does not attack a person merely to hurt and conquer him, but perhaps merely for the pleasure to enjoy one's own instinct.

"That is the most extreme form of nihilism: nothingness ('meaninglessness') eternally!"
Writing from the Late Notebooks[8]

- That is the most extreme form of nihilism: whatsoever ("meaninglessness") eternally!

". . . after coming in contact with a religious man, I always feel that I must wash my hands."
  Ecce Homo[9]

- . . . after coming in contact with a thinker, I always feel that I must "wash" my brain.

"People live for today, people live very fast—people live very irresponsibly: and this is precisely what people call 'freedom'."
  The Twilight of the Idols[10]

- People live for today, people live very fast—people live very irresponsibly: and this is precisely what people call "responsibility".

"Once for all, there is much I do not *want* to know—Wisdom sets bounds even to knowledge."
  —The Twilight of the Idols[11]

- Once for all, there is one thing I do *not* want to know: Wisdom.

"Men press forward to the light not in order to see better but to shine better."
  Human, All Too Human[12]

- Men press forward to the light not in order to see better but to burn better.

**"A tired traveler,
with the hard bark
A dog receives"**
  Nietzsche's Last Notebooks 1888[13]

- A tired dog,
  with the hard bark
  A traveler receives

"And how nicely can the bitch Sensuality knows how to beg for a piece of spirit, when a piece of flesh is denied her!"
Thus Spoke Zarathustra[14]

- And how nicely can the Sensuality of the bitch know how to beg for a piece of spirit, when a piece of flesh is denied her!

**"Truths for our feet,
Truths by which dance can be"**
Nietzsche's Last Notebooks 1888[15]

- Truths for our feet,
  Truths that can have only kicks.

"Insects sting, not from malice, but because they too want to live. It is the same with our critics—they desire our blood, not our pain."
Human, All Too Human[16]

- Insects sting only from malice, they have no consciousness of death. It is the same with our critics—they desire our blood and our pain too.

"Not only doth he lies, who speaketh contrary to his knowledge, but more so, he who speaketh contrary to his ignorance."
Thus Spake Zarathustra[17]

- Not only doth he lies, who speaketh similarly to his knowledge, but more so, he who speaketh similarly to his ignorance.

"I fear you when you are near; I love you when you are far. . ."
Thus Spoke Zarathustra[18]

- I fear you when you are inside me; I love you when you are inside you.

"Uncanny is human existence and still without meaning: a buffoon can be fatal."
Thus Spoke Zarathustra[19]

- Uncanny is human existence and still without meaning: its fate is as a buffoonery.

"When one is misunderstood generally, it is impossible to remove a particular misunderstanding. This point must be recognized, to save superfluous expenditure of energy in self-defense."
Human, All Too Human[20]

- When one is misunderstood . . . This point must be recognized to squander a *goodbye* for our own self-defense.

"The friend whose hopes we cannot satisfy is one we should prefer to have as an enemy."
Daybreak[21]

- The friend whose jealousies we cannot satisfy is one we should prefer to have as an enemy.

"Look at those superfluous! Diseased they ever are, they vomit bile and call it newspaper. They devour but cannot digest each other."
Thus Spoke Zarathustra[22]

- Look at those superfluous! Diseased they ever are, they vomit bile and call it newspaper. They vomit their oneself because they cannot digest each other.

"Learn to laugh at yourselves as one must laugh!"
Thus Spoke Zarathustra[23]

- Laugh to learn on yourselves as one must learn!

"... wisdom is the whispering of the sage to himself in the crowded market-place."

Human, All Too Human[24]

- ... wisdom is the whispering of the sage to himself about himself in any place.

"Pain makes hens and poets cackle."

Thus Spoke Zarathustra[25]

- Jealousy makes peacocks and professors cackle.

"With all things one thing is impossible—rationality!"

Thus Spoke Zarathustra[26]

- With all things one thing is rational: impossibility!

"The sting of conscience, like the gnawing of a dog at a stone, is mere foolishness."

Human, All Too Human[27]

- The sting of conscience, like the shit of a dog at a stone, a necessity.

"That everybody is allowed to learn to read spoileth in the long run not only writing but thinking."

Thus Spake Zarathustra[28]

- That everybody is allowed to learn to think spoileth in the long run not only writing but reading.

"Whoever thinks much is unsuitable for a party-man; his thinking leads him too quickly beyond the party."
Human, All Too Human[29]

- Whoever a party-man pretends he thinks much; his *thinking* leads him too quickly behind the party.

"Those you cannot teach to fly, teach to fall faster."
Thus Spoke Zarathustra[30]

- Those you cannot teach to fly, push them to fall faster.

"Are we not always seated at a great table for play and mockery?"
Thus Spoke Zarathustra[31]

- Are we not always seated at a great table for bet and extort?

"Our duties—these are the rights others have over us."
Dawn[32]

- Our duties—these are the duties of others too.

"Why might not the world *which concern us*—**be a fiction?"**
Beyond Good and Evil[33]

- Why might not the world *which concern the others*—be a fiction?

"But tell me, I pray, my brethren: if the goal be lacking to humanity, is not humanity itself lacking?"
Thus Spake Zarathustra[34]

- But tell me, I pray, my brethren: if the ontology be lacking to humanity, is not humanity's teleology lacking?

"We sometimes remain faithful to a cause merely because its opponents never cease to be insipid."
Human, All Too Human[35]

- We sometimes remain faithful to a cause merely because we are not up to it.

"Many die too late, and some die too early. Still the doctrine soundeth strange: 'Die at the right Time'."
Thus Spake Zarathustra[36]

- Many die too late, and some die too early. Still the doctrine soundeth strange: "Have time to die."

**"Who once wore chains, will always think
That he is followed by their clink."**
The Gay Science[37]

- Who once handcuffed chains, will always think
  That he is followed by their clink.

". . . for whoever has not two-thirds of his day for himself is a slave, be he otherwise whatever he likes, statesman, merchant, official, or scholar."
Human, All Too Human[38]

- . . . for whoever has not two-thirds of his day for himself is a slave of his desires, be he otherwise whatever he likes, statesman, merchant, official, or scholar.

"And ye tell me, friends, that there is to be no dispute about taste and tasting? But all life is a dispute about taste and tasting!"
Thus Spake Zarathustra[39]

- And ye tell me, friends, that there is to be no dispute about feelings and perceptions? But all life is a dispute about feelings and perceptions!

"But how could I be just from the heart! How can I give everyone his own! Let this be enough for me: I give unto every one mine own."
Thus Spake Zarathustra[40]

- But how could I be just from the heart! How can I give everyone his own! Let this be enough for me: I give unto every one the own of the others.

"When one has a great deal to put into it a day has a hundred pockets."
Human, All Too Human[41]

- When one has a great deal to put into it, pockets look for him, daily.

"Thoughts are the shadows of our sentiments."
The Joyful Wisdom[42]

- Sentiments are our thoughts under light.

". . . for mankind has as a whole *no* goals . . ."
Human, All Too Human[43]

- . . . for mankind has as a whole *to change goals* . . .

"To 'give style' to one's character—that is a grand and a rare art!"
The Joyful Wisdom[44]

- To "give style" to one's character—that is a poor and a widespread art!

"'To the clean are all things clean' thus say the people. I, however, say unto you: To the swine all things become swinish!"
Thus Spake Zarathustra[45]

- "To the clean are all things swinish" thus say the people. I, however, say unto you: To the swine all things become clean!

"The object of punishment is to improve him *who punishes* . . . "
The Joyful Wisdom[46]

- The object of punishment is to improve the punishment . . .

"And if all ladders henceforth fail thee, then must thou learn to mount upon thine own head: how couldst thou mount up ward otherwise?"
Thus Spake Zarathustra[47]

- And if your head henceforth fails thee, then must thou learn to descend on any ladder: how couldst thou mount up ward otherwise?

"Nobody is responsible for his actions, nobody for his nature; to judge is identical with being unjust."
Human, All Too Human[48]

- Nobody is responsible for his actions, nobody for his nature; to judge is identical with being playing.

"As soon as a religion triumphs it has for its enemies all those who would have been its first disciples."
Human, All Too Human[49]

- As soon as a religion/party triumphs it has for its enemies all those who would have been its first founders.

"But thus I counsel you, my friends: Mistrust all in whom the impulse to punish is powerful!"
Thus Spake Zarathustra[50]

- But thus I counsel you, my friends: Mistrust all in whom the impulse to punish is intrinsic!

"Vicariousness of the Senses. 'We have also eyes in order to hear with them,'—said an old confessor who had grown deaf; 'and among the blind he that has the longest ears is king.'"
The Joyful Wisdom[51]

- Vicariousness of the Values. "We have also vices in order to reach,"—said an old fart who had become bright; "and among the donkeys he that has the longest ears is human."

"Poet and Liar—The poet sees in the liar his foster-brother whose milk he has drunk up; the latter has thus remained wretched, and has not even attained to a good conscience."
The Joyful Wisdom[52]

- Liar and Poet—The liar sees in the poet his foster-brother whose milk he has drunk up; the latter has thus remained wretched, and has not even attained to a good reputation.

"His compassion is hard,
Pressure crushes his love:
not give a huge hand!"
Nietzsche's Last Notebooks 1888[53]

- His compassion is hard,
Pressure crushes his love:
not give a hand to a dwarf!

"Obstinacy and faithfulness—Obstinately, he clings to something that he has come to see through; but he calls it 'faithfulness'."
The Gay Science[54]

- Obstinacy and faithfulness—Obstinately, he clings to something that he has seen nothing; but he calls it "faithfulness".

"Alas, there are so many things between heaven and earth of which poets only have dreamt!"
Thus Spake Zarathustra[55]

- "Alas, there is nothing things between heaven and earth of which poets only have dreamt!

"Laughable! See! See!—He runs away from men: they follow him, however, because he runs *before* them—they are such a gregarious lot!"
The Joyful Wisdom[56]

- Laughable! See! See!—He is mocking man: they are mocking themselves in return, however, because he is mocking *before* them—they are such a gregarious lot!"

"They have pity on my accidents and chances. But my word is: 'Let chance come unto me! Innocent it is, as a little child!'"
Thus Spake Zarathustra[57]

- They have pity on my accidents and chances. But my chances say: "Let them play with themselves! Innocents they are, as little children!".

"He that has joy abounding must be a good man, but perhaps he is not the cleverest of men, although he has reached the very goal towards which the cleverest man is striving with all his cleverness."
Human, All Too Human[58]

- He that has joy abounding must be a stupid man, but sure he is not the cleverest of men, although he has reached the very goal towards which the cleverest man is striving with all his cleverness. There is no compatibility between cleverness and happiness.

"They still work, for work is an entertainment. But they are careful, lest the entertainment exhaust them."
Thus Spake Zarathustra[59]

- They still work, for work is a form of parrot. But they are careful, lest the parrot exhaust them, relentlessly.

"Bad taste has its rights like good taste . . . "
The Joyful Wisdom[60]

- Bad reason has its rights like good reason . . .

"How can anyone become a thinker if he does not spend at least a third part of the day without passions, men, and books?"
Human, All Too Human[61]

- How can anyone become a thinker if he does not spend at least a third part of the day without men, men and men?

"Too Jewish. If God had wanted to become an object of love, he would first of all have had to forgo judging and justice—a judge, and even a gracious judge, is no object of love."
The Joyful Wisdom[62]

- Too Roman. If Rome had wanted that God to become an object of love, it would first of all have had to forgo judging and justice—a judge, and even a gracious judge, is no object of love.

". . . but he who thinks in *words*, thinks as a speaker and not as a thinker . . . he only thinks of himself and his audience."
   The Genealogy of Morals[63]

- . . . but he who thinks in *feelings*, thinks as a demagogue and not as a thinker . . . he only thinks of himself and the feelings of his audience.

"Behind thy thoughts and feelings, my brother, standeth a mighty lord, an unknown wise man whose name is self. In thy body he dwelleth, thy body he is."
   Thus Spake Zarathustra[64]

- Behind thy thoughts and feelings, my brother, standeth a stupid lord, a well-known donkey whose name is reason. In thy body he dwelleth, thy body he is.

"It is an excellent thing to express; a thing consecutively in two ways, and thus provide it with a right and a left foot. Truth can stand indeed on one leg, but with two she will walk and complete her journey."
   Human, All Too Human[65]

- It is an excellent thing not to express; a thing consecutively in two ways, and thus not to provide it with a right and a left foot. Truth can stand indeed on one leg, and she will piss and complete her journey.

"My brother, if thou hast good luck, thou hast one virtue and no more: thus thou walkest more easily over the bridge."
Thus Spake Zarathustra[66]

- My brother, if thou hast good luck, thou hast one virtue and no more: thus the bridge walkest more easily over you.

"Error has made animals into men; is truth perhaps capable of making man into animal again?"
Human, All Too Human[67]

- Ingratitude has made men into animals; is gratitude perhaps capable of making animals into men again?

"He who lives by fighting with an enemy has an interest in the preservation of the enemy's life."
Human, All Too Human[68]

- He who lives by fighting with an enemy has an interest in the preservation of his own life.

". . . one must do as the traveler who wants to know the height of the towers of a city: for that purpose he leaves the city."
The Joyful Wisdom[69]

- . . . one must do as anyone who did not want to know the height of the towers of a city: for that purpose, he insists to stay in the city.

"Mighty waters sweep many stones and shrubs away with them; mighty spirits many foolish and confused minds."
Human, All Too Human[70]

- Mighty waters sweep many stones and shrubs away with them; mighty spirits sweep away but themselves.

"I have given a name to my pain, and call it 'a dog,'—it is just as faithful, just as importunate and shameless, just as entertaining, just as wise, as any other dog—and I can domineer over it, and vent my bad humor on it, as others do with their dogs, servants, and wives."
The Joyful Wisdom[71]

- I have given a name to my pain, and call it "a dog,"—it is just as unfaithful, but funny and shameless, just as entertaining, just as wise, as any other dog—and it can domineer over me and vent my bad humor, as others do with their dogs: have fun while walking.

"Your great thoughts,
  coming from the heart,
  and all your little
—They come out of my head—
  they are not all bad thought?"
Nietzsche's Last Notebooks 1888[72]

- Your great thoughts,
  coming from the heart,
  and all your little
  —They come out of my head—
  they are not all a *déjà vue*?

"One person sticks to an opinion because he takes pride in having acquired it himself—another sticks to it because he has learnt it with difficulty and is proud of having understood it; both of them, therefore, out of vanity."
Human, All Too Human[73]

- One person sticks to an opinion because he convinced the other that it is his own—because he has learned it with difficulty and is proud of having understood it; therefore, it is out of villainy.

"There is always a madness in love. There is, however, also always a reason in madness."
Thus Spake Zarathustra[74]

- There is but madness in love. There is, however, but reason in madness.

"Fellowship in joy, and not sympathy in sorrow, makes people friends."
Human, All Too Human[75]

- Fellowship in joy, and not sympathy in sorrow, makes yourself friend of yourself.

3
On New Dimensions

"Whatever is done from love always occurs beyond good and evil."
Beyond Good and Evil[1]

- Whatever is done from love always occurs beyond the Hereafter.

"'Go to hell, who goes your way?'—
Well! to my hell [*Hölle*]
I want the road paved with good sayings to me"
Nietzsche's Last Notebooks 1888[2]

- "Go to heaven, who goes your way?"—
  Well! to my heaven
  I want the road paved with suspicious sayings to me.

"All is alike, nothing is worthwhile, the world is without meaning, knowledge strangleth."
Thus Spake Zarathustra[3]

- All is alike, nothing is worthwhile, the world is without meaning, teleology strays.

"Beggars ought to be abolished: for one is vexed at giving to them and vexed at not giving to them."
Daybreak[4]

- Donors ought to be abolished: for one is vexed at taking from them and vexed at not taking from them.

"Thou must be ready to burn thyself in thine own flame: how canst thou become new, if thou hast not first become ashes!"
  Thus Spake Zarathustra[5]

- Thou must be ready to burn the others in thine own flame: how canst thou become new, if thou hast not first made them ashes!

**"Rubble of stars:
from these ruins I make my world"**
  Nietzsche's Last Notebooks 1888[6]

- Rubble of values:
  from these ruins I make my world.

"I have forgotten my umbrella"
  Writing from the Early Notebooks[7]

- I am my umbrella.

"Silent envy grows in silence."
  Human, All Too Human[8]

- Manifested envy subsides in noise.

"I walk among human beings as among fragments of the future: that future which I envisage."
  Ecce Homo[9]

- I walk among human beings as among fragments of the past: that past which I forgot.

"... it was during the years of my lowest vitality that I ceased to be a pessimist..."
Ecce Homo[10]

- ... it was during the years of my lowest vitality that I started having "friends"...

"Men of profound thought appear to themselves in intercourse with others like comedians, for in order to be understood they must always simulate superficiality."
—*Human, All Too Human*[11]

- Men of profound thought appear to themselves in intercourse with others like dumb, for in order to be understood they must always remain silent.

"Once spirit was God, then it became man, and now it is becoming mob."
Thus Spake Zarathustra[12]

- Once man was mob, then it became spirit, and now it is becoming god.

"Your bad love of yourselves makes solitude a prison to you."
Thus Spoke Zarathustra[13]

- Your bad love of your solitude makes yourself the prison of yourself.

"There is an innocence in lying which is the sign of good faith in a cause."
Beyond Good and Evil[14]

- There is an innocence in believing which is the sign of good cause to lie.

"The will to power as *life*."
Writing from the Late Notebooks[15]

- The will to love is *life*.

"Once for all, there is much I do not want to know. - Wisdom sets bounds even to knowledge."
The Twilight of the Idols[16]

- Once for all, there is much I do not to remember. - Wisdom reside in our memory.

"You are running ahead?—Are you doing it as a shepherd? Or as an exception? A third case would be when someone is running away . . . First question of conscience."
The Twilight of the Idols[17]

- You are running ahead?—Are you doing it as a shepherd? Or as an exception? A third case would be when someone is running away . . . A fourth case would be a pretention to be the first. First question of conscience.

"Parmenides said: 'One does not think that which is not'—we are at the other extreme and say: 'what can be thought must certainly be a fiction'. Thinking has no grip on the real, but only on . . ."
Writing from the Late Notebooks[18]

- Parmenides said: "One does not think that which is not"—we are at the same extreme and say: "what can be thought must certainly be a fiction". Thinking has no grip on the real, but only on itself."

"This is the sort of artist I love, modest in his needs: he really only wants two things, his bread and his art—panem et Circen."
The Twilight of the Idols[19]

- This is the sort of artist I love, modest in his needs: he really only wants two things, his art and his art.

"Sleep knocking at mine eye, it getteth heavy. Sleep touching my mouth, it remaineth open. Verily, on soft soles it approacheth me, the dearest of thieves, stealing my thoughts. . ."
Thus Spake Zarathustra[20]

- Sleep knocking at mine eye, it getteth heavy. Sleep touching my mouth, it remaineth open. Verily, on soft soles it approacheth me, the dearest of thieves, inspiring my thoughts. . .

"This call is the result of an insight that I was the first to formulate: *there are absolutely no* **moral facts."**
The Twilight of the Idols[21]

- This call is the result of an insight that I was the first to formulate: *there are absolutely no* more absolutes.

"A Romantic is an artist made creative by his great displeasure with himself—who looks away, looks back from himself and the rest of his world"
Writing from the Late Notebooks[22]

- A Researcher is a scientific made creative by his great displeasure with his achievement—who looks away, looks back from himself and the rest of his world.

"There is more sagacity in thy body than in thy best wisdom."
Thus Spake Zarathustra[23]

- There is less sagacity in thy mind than in thy deepest heart.

"I do not know out or in; I am whatever does not know out or in. . ."
The Anti-Christ[24]

- I do not know out or in; I became whatever does not know what is out to go out. . .

"Wherefore dost thou fear? It is with man as with the tree. The more he would ascend to height and light the stronger are his roots striving earthwards, downwards, into the dark, the deep, the evil."
Thus Spake Zarathustra[25]

- The more he would ascend to height and light the more strongly their aspirations strive to eat the earthward, the downward, the darkness, the depthness: the evil.

"Why should one live? All is vain! To live—that is to thresh straw; to live—that is to burn oneself and yet not get warm."
Thus Spake Zarathustra[26]

- Why should one live? All is vain! To live - that is to thresh straw; to live - that is to burn oneself and let the others get warm.

"The snake that cannot cast its skin perishes. So too with those minds which are prevented from changing their views: they cease to be minds."
The Dawn Of Day[27]

- The snake that cannot cast its skin perishes. So too with those minds which are, continuously, change their views: they cease to be minds.

"Many a man fails to become a thinker for the sole reason that his memory is too good."
Human, All Too Human[28]

• Many a man fails to become a thinker for the sole reason that his consciousness is too conscious.

"Hitherto all that has given colour to existence has lacked a history. . ."
The Joyful Wisdom[29]

• Hitherto all that has given value to existence has lacked a history. . .

"Go ahead and do whatever you will—but first be the kind of people who can will."
Thus Spake Zarathustra[30]

• Go ahead and do whatever you achieve—but first be the kind of people who can achieve.

"'This is now my way, where is yours?' Thus did I answer those who asked me 'the way'. For the way it doth not exist!"
Thus Spake Zarathustra[31]

• "This is now my way, where is yours?" Thus did I answer those who asked me "the way." For the way it has its own way!

"The great advantage of having noble origins is that it enables one more easily to endure poverty."
Daybreak[32]

• The great advantage of having noble Education is that it enables one more easily to endure ignorance.

"I am always among you
like oil in water:
always on top"
Nietzsche's Last Notebooks 1888[33]

- I am always among you
  like oil in water:
  the top always relies on me.

"My paradise lies 'in the shadow of my sword'"
Ecce Homo[34]

- My paradise lies "in the shadow of my pen".

"Thoughts and Words—Even our thoughts we are unable to render
completely in words."
The Joyful Wisdom[35]

- Realities and Words—All realities, tangible or not, too, we are
  unable to render completely in words.

"Lonely days,
you want to go on brave feet!"
Nietzsche's Last Notebooks 1888[36]

- Lonely days,
  you want to go quick steps, towards solitude!

"We forget our fault when we have confessed it to another person, but he
does not generally forget it."
Human, All Too Human[37]

- We feel noble when we renounce our rights, but the others feel
  differently.

"Here there is thunder enough to make even graves learn to listen!"
Thus Spoke Zarathustra[38]

- Here there are graves enough to make thunder learn to rumble!

"Change of values, i. e., change of creators! He who is obliged to be a creator ever destroyeth."
Thus Spake Zarathustra[39]

- Change of values, i. e., change of teachers! He who is obliged to be a teacher ever destroyeth.

". . . the night is also a sun."
Thus Spoke Zarathustra[40]

- The sun is sometimes a sun.

"We sometimes remain faithful to a cause merely because its opponents never cease to be insipid."
Human, All Too Human[41]

- We sometimes remain faithful to a cause merely because it has no opponents.

"A person often does not know how rich he is, until he learns from experience what rich men even play the thief on him."
The Joyful Wisdom[42]

- A person often does not know how rich he is, until he learns from experience how thief men became honest due to him.

"Into my bone:
'world has no heart,
And stupid he, who'd therefore groan!'"
    The Gay Science[43]

- Into my heart:
  "world has no bone,
  And wise he, who'd therefore groan!"

". . . unequal rights are the condition for any rights at all."
    The Anti-Christ[44]

- . . . unequal rights are the condition for any condition to be.

"The only thing that cannot be refused to these poor beasts of burden is their 'holidays'—such is the name they give to this ideal of leisure in an overworked century; 'holidays', in which they may for once be idle, idiotic and childish to their heart's content."
    The Dawn Of Day[45]

- The only thing that cannot be allowed to these poor beasts of burden is their "holidays"—such is the name they give to this ideal of leisure in an overworked century; "holidays", in which they even are not allowed to enjoy being for once idle, idiotic and childish to their heart's content.

". . . after all, a dancer has ears in his toes!"
    Thus Spoke Zarathustra[46]

- . . . after all, a singer has ears in his feelings!

"... art did not simply imitate the reality of nature but rather supplied a metaphysical supplement to the reality of nature, and was set alongside the latter as a way of overcoming it."
The Birth of Tragedy[47]

- ... art did not simply negate the reality of nature but rather supplied a metaphysical subtraction to the reality of nature, and was set alongside the latter as a way of overcoming each other.

"What do you love in others?—My hopes."
The Gay Science[48]

- What do you hope in others?—My love.

"The one who is punished is no longer the one who did the deed. He is always the scapegoat."
Dawn[49]

- The one who is punished is no longer the one who did the deed. He is always the one who defends us.

"One repays a teacher badly if one always remains a pupil only."
Thus Spoke Zarathustra[50]

- One repays a teacher badly if he does not become again his pupil.

"The advantage of a bad memory is that one enjoys several times the same good things for the first time."
Human, All Too Human[51]

- The advantage of a bad memory is that one forgets several times the same bad things for several time.

"Whoever has not got a good father should procure one."
Human, All Too Human[52]

- Whoever does not have a good father should make him his child.

"A man far oftener appears to have a decided character from persistently following his temperament than from persistently following his principles."
Human, All Too Human[53]

- A man far oftener appears to have a decided character from persistently showing his temperament than from persistently showing his principles.

"Poet and Liar—The poet sees in the liar his foster-brother whose milk he has drunk up; the latter has thus remained wretched, and has not even attained to a good conscience."
The Joyful Wisdom[54]

- Liar and Philosopher—The liar sees in the philosopher his foster-brother whose milk he has drunk up; the latter has thus remained wretched, and has not even attained to a one answer.

"The reader offers a twofold insult to the author by praising his second book at the expense of his first (or *vice versa*) and by expecting the author to be grateful to him on that account."
Human, All Too Human[55]

- The person offers a twofold insult to the other human by praising his second service at the expense of his first (or *vice versa*) and by expecting him to be grateful to him on that account.

"Out of obstinacy he holds fast to a cause of which the questionableness has become obvious—he calls that, however, his 'loyalty.'"
The Joyful Wisdom[56]

- Out of conviction he holds fast to a cause of which has become logocentric—he calls that, however, his "loyalty".

"Now I am light, now I fly, now I see myself beneath myself, now a God danceth through me."
Thus Spake Zarathustra[57]

- Now I am light, now I fly, now I see myself inside yourself, true Friedrich, now a God danceth within you.

"Ten truths a day thou must find: else thou seekest for truth even in the night, thy soul having remained hungry."
Thus Spake Zarathustra[58]

- Ten truths a day thou must find: as well as ten truths even in the night, thy soul having remained hungry.

"Towards my goal I struggle, mine own way I go; I shall overleap those who hesitate and delay. Let my way be their destruction!"
Thus Spake Zarathustra[59]

- Towards me, my goal struggles, its own way it goes; it shall overleap those who hesitate and delay. Let its way be its glory!

"You can change a brazen duty into gold in the eyes of all by always performing something more than you have promised."
Human, All Too Human[60]

- You can change a brazen duty into gold in the eyes of all by always performing more than one expected and more than one can never expect.

"A book full of intellect communicates something thereof even to its opponents."
Human, All Too Human[61]

- A book full of foolishness communicates something thereof even to its partisans.

"wherever he went? who knows?
but it is certain that he downfall (untergieng).
A star went out in the desert space:
bleak was the room. . ."
Nietzsche's Last Notebooks 1888[62]

- wherever he went? I know.
  but it is certain that he downfall [untergieng].
  A star lost out in the desert space:
  night was a desert of bright stars. . .

"I love those who do not know how to live unless in perishing, for they are those going beyond."
Thus Spake Zarathustra[63]

- I love those who do not know how to live unless in perishing, for their presence shines through their absence.

"Here is a hero who did nothing but shake the tree as soon as the fruits were ripe. Do you think that too small a thing? Well, just look at the tree that he shook."
Human, All Too Human[64]

- Here is a hero who did nothing but look at the tree as soon as the fruits were ripe. Do you think that too small a thing? Well, just look at the fruits of the tree.

"Many a man adds a bit of his personality to his bad arguments, as if they would thus go better and change into straight and good arguments. In the same way, players at skittles, even after a throw, try to give a direction to the ball by turns and gestures."
Human, All Too Human[65]

- Many a man adds a bit of his personality to his bad arguments, as if they would thus go better and change into straight and good arguments. In the same way, players at Horse Racing Courses, even after the departure, try to jump, jump and jump.

"The wheel and the drag have different duties, but also one in common— that of hurting each other."
Human, All Too Human[66]

- The alcohol and my brain have different duties, but also one in common—that to relief one another.

"Without cruelty, no feast: so teaches the oldest and longest history of man—and in punishment too is there so much of the *festive*."
A Genealogy of Morals[67]

- Without trade, no feast: so teaches the oldest and longest history of man—and in loss too is there so much of the *festive*.

"A single joyless person is enough to make constant displeasure and a clouded heaven in a household; and it is only by a miracle that such a person is lacking!—Happiness is not nearly such a contagious disease;— how is that?"
The Joyful Wisdom[68]

- A single ambitionless person is enough to make constant displeasure and a clouded heaven in a household; and it is only by a miracle that such a person is lacking!—Responsibility is not nearly such a contagious disease;—how is that?"

"He who is unassuming toward people manifests his presumption all the more with regard to things (town, State, society, time, humanity). That is his revenge."
Human, All Too Human[69]

- He who is unassuming toward profanes people manifests his presumption all the more with regard to initiated people. That is his revenge.

"He who speaks a foreign language imperfectly has more enjoyment therein than he who speaks it well. The enjoyment is with the partially initiated."
Human, All Too Human[70]

- He who knows to do a task imperfectly has more enjoyment therein than he who does it well. The enjoyment is with the profane, continuously to prove a self-esteem.

"he had collected himself after,
He was already tired,
he already looks the way he went -
and more recently he loved everything untrodden (Unbegangne)!"
Nietzsche's Last Notebooks 1888[71]

- he had collected himself after,
  He was already tired,
  he already regains the way he went -
  and more recently he loved everything trodden even by himself!

"The whole of beautiful art and of great art belongs here their common essence is gratitude."
The case of Wagner[72]

- The whole of beautiful All and of Great All belongs here their common essence is gratitude.

"**What dost thou Believe in?—In this: That the weights of all things must be determined anew.**"
The Joyful Wisdom[73]

* What dost thou Believe in?—In this: That the weightless is nothing.

"**Nobody dies nowadays of fatal truths, there are too many antidotes to them.**"
Human, All Too Human[74]

* Nobody dies nowadays of fatal truths, there are but much pretentiousness.

"*The Realistic Painter*
'To all of nature true!'—How does he plan?
Would nature fit an image *made by man*?
The smallest piece of world is infinite!—
He ends up painting that which he *sees fit*.
And what does he see fit? Paint what he *can*!"
The Gay Science[75]

* The Utopian Thinker
  "True to his convictions!"—How does he plan?
  Would reason fit a conviction *made by man*?
  The smallest piece of his mind's cells is infinite!—
  He ends up reasoning that which he *sees fit*.
  And what does he see fit? Reasoning what he *can*!

II

FRIEDRICH, ARE MY ETERNAL
THOUGHTS RECURRENT?

1
Friedrich, Enjoy!

1   We invented the laugh to mock his teeth.

2   We invented the festivals to mock at our clothes and our behaviors.

3   We invented the clothes to see better our organs.

4   We invented History to re-questioning the chronology of time.

5   We invented celebrations as agreements made between different traders to organize and plan the items for sale.

6   We invented the makeup to let the other taste, elsewhere.

7   We invented the incense to not die from of our odors.

8   We invented the details to waste time.

9   We invented the occult sciences to despise reason.

10 We invented the alcohol to allow us to understand the inexplicable things.

11 We invented the burials to clear the space!

12 We invented the real reality to corrupt a beautiful virtual one!

13 We invented sex to learn the reality of disgust.

14 We invented the future to mock at our past.

15 We invented the mechanical science to mock of one muscles!

16 We invented the age to let our achievement despise us!

17 We invented music to communicate without understanding and therefore to understand what we want.

18 We invented the jewelry to hide our wrinkles.

19 We invented the immigration to take revenge on our parents.

20 God invented the reproduction to showcase our ingratitude.

21 We invented entertainment to escape our heads.

22 We invented the self esteem in order to be able to enjoy fucking ourselves.

23 We invented the defense to allow to the members of the jury to attack each others.

24 We invented the power in order to reveal our real own reality.

25 We invented the cosmetic surgeries not to be more beautiful but to mock and revenge from our genes and to aggravate, with traces, our own ugliness.

26 We invented the gloves to avoid dirtying our environment.

27 We invented Mathematics to confirm logocentrism.

28 We invented candles on the cake in the birthdays to let the celebrated, when he extinguishes the candles, spit on the cake in order to eat it alone!

29 We invented the conferences to use stakeholders to beg.

30 We have invented forgetfulness to harm our happiness.

31 We invented the marriage to perpetuate between love and friendship.

32 We invented the teamwork in order to blame each other when mistakes occur and to monopolize success when it is completed.

33 We invented the language for not to express our feelings but to hide them.

34 We invented the net (the ease of access to information) to increase ignorance.

35 We invented the various saints to enable the sinners, every time they sin, on request, to change the solicitation.

36 We invented the actor to allow him to live his real life.

37 We invented the dance to excite ourselves, officially, in front of everyone.

38 We invented hats to increase the sizes of the brain!

39 We invented writing in order to clear our heads and give way to other ideas.

40 We have invented the truth to shame our apologies.

41 We invented colorless tears so that we can cry as much as we want without knowing how much we have cried!

42 We invented public places not to increase the social interaction but to attract the voyeurs!

43 We invented pedophilia to reward the pores of the woman's skin.

44 We invented the disguising to show our real reality.

45 We invented theories to replace five-star prisons.

46 We invented the elasticity of time to experiment the feeling of love before and after separation.

47 We invented the Anniversary to falsify the irregular cycle of the universe.

48 We invented *illogism* to help thinkers to solve unsolved problems.

49 We invented the memory in order to continuously feel guilty.

50 We invented the low-waist to enable women to be more sexy, but from above.

51 We invented the News not to inform people but to distort them.

52 We invented the acts, rites, and cults of a belief to increase the belief : the raison d'être of the clown.

53 We invented the concerts to expect whom, among the musicians, will go wrong first.

54 We invented the choir in the church because the priest is boring.

55 We invented the devil to exploit the saints! And the saints invented the angels so that, in turn, they exploit us.

56 We invented loneliness not to escape the others but escape ourselves.

57 We invented the concept of instinct for animals to justify human behavior.

58 We invented the stairs to tease the elderly!

59 We invented the friendship to fuck his friend! And we invented the fuck to make friends! And we were in need to invent to enjoy seeing fucking!

60 We invented balls sports, to have the excuse, with our muscles, to hit the others.

61 We invented money with two extremely different faces, drawing inspiration from men.

62 We invented theories to let knowledge be less boring.

63 We invented the glasses to hide tears as much as smiles!

64 We invented the earrings to derive attention to the ugliness of the face.

65 We invented the guilds to organize the robbery.

66 We invented agriculture for lazy people.

67 We invented the long meetings to tease smokers.

68 We invented the notebook to betray our memory.

69 We invented dreams to get rid of life.

70 We invented terminologies to humiliate the initiated and not the profanes.

71 We invented the invitations to test the greed of others.

72 We invented free time to liberate time!

73 We invented the rhythm (biological, environmental, music, etc.) in order to prevent people from enjoying freedom and subsequently to become its slave.

74 We invented the fire for people to learn gratitude. As much as one gives, as much as one receives!

75 We invented the calendar, the clock, etc., not to follow the rhythm of the universe but to let the universe follows our needs!

76 We invented silence to allow to our thoughts to scream.

77 We invented philosophy to escape the difficulty of science.

78 We invented the values to tease our desires!

79 We invented desires to keep us from knowing our real need.

80 We invented the cynicism to show that dogs are far superior!

81 We invented puppets to save other real puppet!

82 We invented the exceptions of the rule to re-question the rationale of the rule itself.

83 We invented the diplomas so that the pupils would stop learning!

84 We invented the soft drink to delineate the portion of food.

85 We invented the service to allow the servant to despise the service and those who are served.

86 We invented ideas so that they came alone, in secret, to invent us!

87 We invented the jump (jumping) to say that we do not move only step by step!

88 We invented the hookah to let people enjoy watching us sucking!

89 We invented the plates to delimitate our portions.

90 We invented the conversation to prevent people from thinking.

91 We invented the sauce to hide the real taste!

92 We invented loneliness to not die from communication.

93 We invented computers to let the physicians of pain to work.

94 We invented sorrow for wasting time.

95 We invented heights made by man (walls, roofs, skyscrapers, etc.,), aspiring the heights made by nature (trees, rocks, mountains, etc.,), to remind us to become "monkey" again.

96 We invented excuses to escape from other excuses!

97 We invented the power to be satisfied from our self-destruction!

98 We invented the machine to let it tell us: "I, machine, I think, and you man, you apply!"

99 We invented the illusions to mock from our perception and our cognition.

100 We invented the position to allow to the others to hate us.

2
Friedrich, Think a Little Bit!

1   The love for the lover is the degree of honesty and nobility that has a person to himself. Love, has nothing to do to the lover!

2   We look for problems or the problems seek us. The problem is only for one who seek first!

3   When one ceases to search, what we seek come to beg us to seek him again, barefoot!

4   Who said that peace was always the way to keep peace?

5   Forgetting an idea is a grace.

6   Even pity has its rules and regulations. It is not arbitrary!

7   The term «beautiful» is a term hides behind it what we could not express in language.

8   Whoever had been the most mistaken thinks the most.

9   Belonging is a pragmatic need even Machiavellian. We belong to what suits us and not to ones we should belong!

10 The tools of a cause are not always made to support it but sometimes to forget it.

11 Our lament comes only from what we have decided ourselves before.

12 It is not always those who betray us that are guilty!

13 Habit is a single-edged weapon. Always against oneself.

14 Decision? A choice that has not take into consideration other decisions!

15 Go ahead, I encourage you, do not look back; but remember that every back is always a new front.

16 Heraclites, be careful, it's not only the water that changes!

17 Charlatanism arises only in developed societies.

18 In songs, there are words that can even hypnotize the music and there is music can hypnotize the words.

19 The second person in any party is the most attacked because either he is well prepared to be attacked or he deserves to be well attacked. It remains one case: to make the attacks his own game. This is the rule to predict the continuity of all parties.

20 The avid helps people when they find them more at rest while the disinterested help the avid to work more.

21 The value of money depends on ours. As far as one is great it is and as far as one is small it is, too. Our value raises and lowers any medium.

22 The idea is a concept that feels! She flees when it feels negligence!

23 Accessories are rewards to what we are, and we did not want to show them.

24 Decide, and everything will be according to your decision. Especially your desires.

25 Often we admire what is incomprehensible!

26 We are prisoners of our thoughts and the thoughts that will come.

27 It is not the gestures that excite us, but it is the absence of gestures!

28 Every time we have the misery, our senses regress and the senses of others expand!

29 Those who do not have feelings for the others they do not have also for themselves. They think that feelings are obstacles in their path. They

forget that barriers need feelings for cede the pathways.

30 Finally, all wars are due to «experiment» of new physiological needs.

31 If prostitution is to «sell» the body for services; is there a job that prevent us from selling our body for a service? So!!!

32 It is not the addiction to alcohol what matter but it is the addiction to what happened while and after drinking. It is a tool and not an aim.

33 The deprived will be more deprived when he becomes favorite.

34 The problems that confess our friends are not theirs but they are our own problems!

35 Any tendency to wealth is a tendency towards an unnoticed poverty (or noticed thereafter)!

36 The most disgusting is the duty and the more appetizing it is the duty of what we had to do a duty.

37 It's hard to live a lie but what is worse is when we admit that it is a lie!

38 When cheating in exams successfully is willfully, the stupid and conscious will to pay with no return.

39 Neither of approaching or going away from the truth that we can know it, it is only by exceeding it.

40 I'm not in. My games are different and they have rules that have not been fixed yet !

41 The dog chooses the suitable place to shit while man shits everywhere!

42 Mondays are needed, like «I forgot my umbrella».

43 The comfort of sitting on a seat of a toilet is much better than sitting on a seat of a throne.

44 The members of parties and the parties have different aims. The question is: how parties win?

45 The subtlety of our governors is to deviate the teleology of our requests!

46 People who stay in our heads are those who do not see our heads.

47 The stupid institutions need stupids to show their ingenuity!

48 The virtual reality is not necessary a non physical one. It could be too physical, and too real, but our perception was too virtual.

49 We can not learn neither the intelligence nor the stupidity. We can not even teach them. One can only be one of the two, or both, simultaneously!

50 When a thinker finally discovers his own profession he discovers the ontology of his happiness too.

51 We close our eyes when we pray, when we cry, when we dream, when we kiss because we know that the pleasure relies on what to hope to feel to be and not what we feel in reality.

52 The only task of a friend and a lover is to fill the free time to those who already have enough time to fill.

53 The rules are not made only to enable us to cheat! And to cheat is to liberate the rules!

54 Everyone is worth what he wanted to appear in the future and not what he has forgot to show what he can appear!

55 With age, our abilities and capabilities (perceptual and cognitive) decrease; but what increase is our ability to be capable.

56 «Keep beside» knowledge is to say «hold back»! All we guard beside is a past.

57 Man does not accept a foul smell. However, he loves his own. Is disgusting eclectic? Or the eclecticism is disgusting?

58 What we pay him is equal to the one we use to pay.

59 The fallacy is the formula for success. Success is only a falsehood to be formula. The formulas are successful falsehoods.

60 Always, historically, the employees have strategies more adequate than the employers, to resist. No bourgeois still bourgeois, no feudal still feudal, etc., but no employee change its status.

61 A funeral are like receptions. The only difference is that in the funeral we are more comfortable!

62 The woman's tears are a logo centric system of signs which offer the strongest evidence for post structuralist. We can never decipher them because they deny all kinds of communications!

63 Is it the will to look for or the will to forget ourselves?

64 Certainty is a curse of a certain unease of a certain disease.

65 Blessed are the stupids—their stupidity resides in their continuous stupidity. Blessed are the intelligents—their intelligence resides in their continuous stupidity.

66 Whoever invites you wants to insult you.

67 In the frequentation of mediocre we often found intelligent men! Intelligent of «pure wool» mediocre!

68 Why things were kept as souvenirs for a long while realizing that only they serves to almost nothing? Why we insist to keep new souvenirs as well?

69 There are thoughts that are only ornaments and ornaments which are only thoughts!

70 Innovation in sex is a way to hide his disability.

71 Are our experiences our stimuli to think, or is it they limit our thoughts?

72 It was previously said that «Knowledge is in the world», later on, it was realized that «the world is in knowledge». Today it is certain that: knowledge exceeds knowledge.

73 To justify we use all. Even our own honesty.

74 Youth against maturity: muscle against thinking! Why is life made to prevent them from being together?

75 The absence? Only the absence is always present!

76 It's not always that the saint who makes a miracle, sometimes the miracle made a saint!

77 Our existence is to just count our deaths? And then waiting for our turn to be counted by others?

78 Nothing happens to you except what you insist to look for it to happen to you.

79 The difference between what we are hoping to be happened and what we are searching to be happened is that the first is planed but not necessarily we will reach it and the second that we are constantly trying to reach it without any planning!

80 Those who live in history admire people who live there. However, their future will not remain in any history.

81 God has created man to accommodate his head. He has become a headache.

82 The force is when changing the rules and the tools to be stronger. It is the same for thinkers and thoughts.

83 The most subtle way to harm someone is to let him always think about himself.

84 Relive the beautiful memories is more beautiful than reliving in reality.

85 What we negate it publicly is what we love to hide it! To announce is to reject ourselves.

86 The nobility is not hereditary or genetic, nor a selected will but it is a "habit".

87 There are people who are ungrateful even to the devil himself!

88 Man comes to earth without will and goes without will. He lives too without will!

89 The virtues who like to bury themselves are the more who like to remain faithful to themselves.

90 Whoever intends to change the rules he must be sure that his new rules have the power to change him.

91 Any institution (even religious) who suffered persecution from the outset has always need of rites and worship for persecution.

92 For the elderly, recent memories remain, and seem more important than the ancient. Conversely to common sense.

93 Love begins with age neglecting the reality, we live in illusions. Thereafter, gradually we tend towards reality, finally, again, to escape reality. In terms of love, the reality cedes!

94 The goal which requires us to live in hiding ceases to be a goal.

95 The statues are made to insult what they represent.

96 All the advancement in technology can not overcome our rudimentary tools. Were we smarter?

97 Excuses are arguments worse than lies.

98 I don't buy anymore. The value of all that I do not have exceeds all what has price.

99 Does the linguistic accent depend on geography or it is the geography that dependent on the accent?

100 You only die when your will decide to die.

3
Friedrich, It Is Useless to Think!

1   Nil is allowed to borrow my mind from my mind, even my own desires. Paradoxically again, nil is allowed to stop my desires, even my own mind! An eternal debate!

2   When you stop to count your achievements it will be time to forget to re-count again!

3   We choose the viewfinder not for his performance but for his lack of mercy!

4   The fact that all existence has always a past it proves that any existence continues to exist. Past, present and future are mere ornaments for the language!

5   In our relationships, we always think about what others think of us, we rarely think of what our mind thinks of us.

6   What we lack in our former friends, it is not their "effort" to offer us happiness but it is their destitution we continue to offer them!

7   The grimaces are gestures borrowed from animals to show them their humanism!

8   The exploitation is not a quality for those who want to win but for those who know and announce how they will fall.

9   The difference between the conviction and the belief is that in the former there is no doubt.

10   There are laughs that help us to solve problems and there are tears to worsen them.

11   He who lives "a lot" lives "little." and he who lives "little" lives "a lot." Quality and quantity are eternal enemies.

12 We have to play with our desires from time to time. To prevent them; to give them more; it is a test which must be done continuously.

13 When we used to lie to justify ourselves, we have to be up to our lie, otherwise even our lie will humiliate us!

14 People who are alike become profoundly friends. Subsequently, after the separation, they become deeply enemies! Enigmatic issue of human ontology!

15 Unconsciousness is more awake than our consciousness. It is our guardian angel. It arouses us to look where our consciousness refuses to seek and it prevents us from doing what our conscience arouses us to do.

16 No one can be worthy of our grief or our joy. We continually betray them!

17 The loss is a privilege for the « loser ». What is lost does not deserve to be a gain!

18 A past that "passes" worth to be a past that "passed" a lot of pasts with it! Much better for its past, too.

19 To think is to divulge our own secrets to ourselves!

20 When your achievement exceeds your hope and your estimation for yourself then you become a human.

21 All that is incredible is sometimes the most adequate to believe.

22 As far as we think and enjoy as much as we noticed the lack of self-esteem. The need for self-esteem is something that is against our self-esteem!

23 Tears are not begging for pity but to give it.

24 Terror: remember one of our ideas! And do not remember one of our ideas!

25 It is not those who have succeeded that deserve to be judges for success.

26 Cynicism is watching from afar, our head, and try to think without our will!

27 If the famous, in history, were chosen by elites; the elites were chosen by whom?

28 The bridges are not made to cross but to control those who want to cross them. This is valid also for the smile too.

29 Pay from oneself or pay ourselves: it is a waste!

30 Life is a ruin, so everyone should be either a destructor or a tourist!

31 Is our brain responsible for all the behavior of our body? If so, how is it assumed responsibility for committed mistakes? And if not, how isn't it aware of order?

32 Those who do not master a language, their thoughts, in that language are deeper than those whom master it.

33 The gifts are not to reward the sense of deprivation but to increase it.

34 Sometimes we want to play with the same childhood games to simply feel the same sense of unhappiness.

35 Degradation in the body, with age, does not tell what we experienced, but what we wanted to live.

36 The ontology of the tools of war, throughout history, has changed their teleologies.

37 «The apple does not fall far from the tree». And when it does not fall, it casts its shadow on the entire tree.

38 «No one has the right to ignore the law». It is a rule made by "justice" so that it can catch us and then flee.

39 The apogee of a stupidity is to mock of oneself on a committed fault, and at the same time, we hope it will resume!

40 When ideas pass one after the other, it is hard to catch them all, and the worst to you allow them run behind.

41 The intuition is to have much knowledge on anything but in a scattered way.

42 The convictions are poisons; they kill us at their adaptations while doubts are drugs that heals us continually!

43 The pragmatism of the student is always smarter than the vengeance of the teacher!

44 Begging is arriving. Giving is also arriving! Doing nothing is also arriving further!

45 Women search for men who have principles in order to show them that they agree to betray their own principles!

46 Trust is giving everything except our judgment about this everything we gave.

47 The price of time is relative, as well as the price of relative!

48 To improve humanity one must say: like son like father.

49 When doing any ceremony we begin to think about what others want to criticize in order to avoid it. Often we forget what we love, we will end up to like what others like!

50 Whom they ask to be loyal, in fact they are asking their own need to serve you.

51 We measure the degree of intelligence of the other depending on the degree of our. How could we measure ours?

52 In exams, it is not the teacher who «examine» the students, but it is the complete opposite that occurs.

53 The price we pay to realize a hope, is always more than the hope itself. It is realized only when that hope will be achieved!

54 We pray only when we want God to correct his values and not to forgive us.

55 The lack of a real support made of any real restraints a support.

56 The inventors of games grasped their strategies from life itself: attractions, non-predictability, surprises, challenges, defeat, addictions, etc. It's the same strategy adopted by God to create life.

57 How to stop my head from bothering me? Don't I have the right to have a stubborn tranquility?

58 Why, throughout history, we could not find what higher consciousness, but only we have found many ways to lose consciousness?

59 When we know why we are unhappy, we ceased to be! The cause, too, could be the consequence of its effect!

60 In the commitment, there is always either the prison or a freedom. The commitment will be successful when freedom is in an adequate prison.

61 Any abstraction is to indicate what we have not been able to express, but any tangibility is what we had to lie.

62 They climb to arrive; or to get you down; or to not follow your steps because they are afraid to touch the ground to which you have walked.

63 Nobody leaves us (elsewhere or for beyond) without notifying in advance. Often we pretend, deliberately, not to be notified!

64 Addiction is to fight against the memory as well as to struggle with the memory! We drink to forget and we end up by drinking to remember!

65 Couples should not be different. Otherwise, there will be someone who suffers in secret, and the other shows his suffering «happily».

66 The good we do for others it is salvageable? Is it a duty? Is it a gift? Is it a debt for someone else? Or it is an unconscious habit?

67 The gratitude has nothing to do with time; ingratitude the same!

68 Any decision is the result of a conflict between our conscience and our instincts. The right decision is when the conscience fights for instincts and the instincts transcend!

69 As far as we know, as far as we have questions. And if we do not know, we have m less questions? This means that if one strives to know is to strive to ignore!

70 With age, the senses also become mature. They «choose» what to perceive!

71 In seeking the raison d'être of things, we are content that soothes us. Knowing the cause does not calm us but makes us suffer more.

72 To forget one must not stop thinking but to think deeply.

73 Interests change convictions and convictions change principles and principles are "chosen" to defend interests!

74 Institutions benefit to honor famous people, to honor themselves. They always need blood to live.

75 Everyone has his own judgment to categorize humans. And every categorization has its own too!

76 Every great pleasure does not remain long while the small pleasure resist!

77 For atheists: the belief in the dignity is the belief in God himself.

78 In the age of «ambiguity» lies the secret of the advancement of science and knowledge. This is not the case for ages of certainties!

79 We discover «truths» or by reasoning or by perception (the positivists); or by the help of the affection (the phenomenologists). It remains a case: not to try to discover them: they appear by themselves!

80 In seeking an intended goal, we found other goals in passing. And when seeking many goals at once, we found nothing. Is it the nothing always is the goal?

81 Chance is what happens to us as we hoped, unconsciously, to be happened. But, when it happens, we will be surprised, consciously.

82 The child forgets from time to time he is a child, and sometimes he remembers that he is, more!

83 When in heights we forget the various Forms of Smallness. One remembers only their Methods!

84 Our ideas are explosive. If they stay they blow us and if they go out they explode the others.

85 Change his appearance is not to say that one is annoyed at himself, but to prove to ourselves that we are always ourselves in any appearance.

86 Generosity is not giving from what we have, or from we set apart, but to give from what we have not yet . . . from our anything.

87 Astrologers claim that planets control the destiny of human and scientists claim to control the destiny of the planets. Misery pretensions!

88 The strategy of forgetting is to figure out the «forgetfulness» organs and to forget them.

89 What we used to do with dissatisfaction it necessitates little bit a dissatisfaction to be satisfied!

90 Short memory is far wiser than the long memory!

91 We know more people who are far away that people who are close to us!

92 The degree of evaluation grows with maturity and not necessarily with age. It is not a question of experience but of honesty.

93 Marriage? We lose a person or we win another? No, we stay the same number!

94 Anybody can steal our slogans, our principles, our convictions, but never our determination!

95 All that remains is your luck! Make it your God and pray.

96 Happiness is having a mind that is content to have fun with itself.

97 There are people who only have but assertions and people who have none. The latest even doubted from their existence and the first doubted from the doubt itself.

98 The true politician is not the one who can know what will happen but whoever guesses what happened!

99 Ingratitude is a gratitude to ingratitude!

100 When an "author" declares he finished his book it should not be read!

End

"To my Reader.
Good teeth and a digestion good
I wish you these you need, be sure!
And, certes, if my book you've stood,
Me with good humor you'll endure."
  The Joyful Wisdom[1]

- To Friedrich Nietzsche.
  Good teeth and a digestion good
  I wish you these you need, be sure!
  And, certes, if my book you've stood,
  Me with good regret you'll endure.

"Now I am light, now I fly, now I see myself beneath me, now a god dances
through me."
  Thus Spake Zarathustra[2]

- Now I am light, now I fly, now I see myself beneath me, now a
  god dances for me.

"My writings have been called a School for Suspicion."
  Human, All Too Human[3]

- They will use my suspicions as a scholarly book.

"Aphorism and the sentence, in which I, as the foremost among the Germans, am master, are the forms of "eternity; " my ambition is to say in ten sentences what everyone else says in a book—what everyone else does not say in a book. . ."
The Twilight of the Idols[4]

- Aphorism and the sentence, in which I, as the foremost among the Scholars, am master, are the forms of "eternity; " my ambition is to say in ten books what everyone else stipulates to say in one sentence—what everyone else does *not* digest any sentence. . .

"No letters to write!
no books to read!
into the café to take something to read! (ins Café etwas mitnehmen zum Lesen!)
Notebook (Notizbuch!)!"
Nietzsche's Last Notebooks 1888[5]

- No letters to write!
 no books to read!
 into the café to take something to read!
 my book, Friedrich!

"'Having spoken these words Zarathustra again looked at the folk and was silent'. There they are standing, 'he said unto his heart', there they are laughing: they do not understand me, I am not the mouth for these ears."
Thus Spake Zarathustra[6]

- "Having spoken these words, Younes again looked at the folk and was silent." There is he standing, "he said unto his heart", there he is laughing: Nietzsche does not understand me, I am not the mouth for these ears.

"Schopenhauer (. . .) frowned for frowning's sake; from inclination; that he would become sick, become pessimist, (. . .), but for his enemies. . ."
A Genealogy of Morals[7]

- "Nietzsche (. . .) frowned for frowning's sake; from inclination; that he would become sick, become pessimist, (. . .), but for me. . .

"They are so cold, these scholars!
That lightning was beating in their food!
That they learned to eat fire!"
Nietzsche's Last Notebooks 1888[8]

- You are so cold, my scholar!
  That lightning was beating in your food!
  That you learned to eat me!

"God is dead: but as the human race is constituted, there will perhaps be caves for millenniums yet, in which people will show his shadow."
The Joyful Wisdom[9]

- Nietzsche is dead: but as the human race is constituted, there will perhaps be caves for millenniums yet, in which his Superhuman, me for instance, will show his shadow.

"It cannot be helped—every master has but one pupil, and he becomes disloyal to him, for he also is destined for mastery."
Human, All Too Human[10]

- It cannot be helped—every master has but one pupil, and he becomes disloyal to him, for he also is destined for mastery. Here I am, master ! *A la prochaine.*

Notes

Notes of the Beginning:
[1] 1989, Why I Am a Destiny, 1, translated by Walter Kaufmann, edited, with commentary by Walter Kaufmann, Vintage Books, New York.
[2] 1924, *The Complete Works of Friedrich Nietzsche, Volume Ten*, Book Third, 269, edited by Dr Oscar Levy, translated by Thomas Common, With Poetry rendered by Paul V. Cohen and Maude D. Petre, The Macmillan Company, New York.
[3] 1911, *The Complete Works of Friedrich Nietzsche, Volume Seventeen*, Why I Am So Wise, 7, edited by Dr. Oscar Levy, translated by Anthony M. Ludovici, Poetry Rendered by: Paul V. Cohen, Herman Scheffauer, Francis Bickley, Dr. G.T. Wrench, The Macmillan Company, New York.
[4] 1911, *The Complete Works of Friedrich Nietzsche, Volume Seventeen*, Why I Write Such Excellent Books, 1, Edited by Dr. Oscar Levy, translated by Anthony M. Ludovici, Poetry Rendered by: Paul V. Cohen, Herman Scheffauer, Francis Bickley, Dr. G.T. Wrench, The Macmillan Company, New York.
[5] 2007, The Anti-Christ, Ecce Homo, The Twilight of the Idols, and Other Writing, Arrows and Epigrams, 15, edited by Aaron Ridley and Judith Norman, translated by Judith Norman, (First published 2005), Cambridge University Press, Cambridge.
[6] 1917, Zarathustra's Prologue, 5, translated by Thomas Common, the Modern Library, New York.
[7] 2006, Second Part, The Stillest Hour, edited by Adrian Del Caro and Robert Pippin, translated by Adrian Del Caro, Cambridge University Press, New York.
[8] 1911, Part II, Part II, The Wanderer and His Shadow, 121, A Vow, Translated by Paul V. Cohen, B.A., The Macmillan Company, New York.
[9] 1974, Joke, Cunning, and Revenge, 7, Vademecum – Vadetecum, translated, with commentary, by Walter Kaufmann, Vintage Books, New York.
[10] 1924, *The Complete Works of Friedrich Nietzsche, Volume Ten*, Book Third, 255, edited by Dr Oscar Levy, translated by Thomas Common, With Poetry Rendered by Paul V. Cohen and Maude D. Petre, The Macmillan Company, New York.

Notes of the Chapter I:
[1] 1989, *Part Four, Epigrams and Interludes*, 183, translated, with Commentary, by Walter Kaufmann, Vintage Books, A division of Random House, Inc., New York.
[2] 2008, *Book Three*, 267, edited by Bernard Williams, translated by Josefine Nauck-hoff, Poems translated by Adrian Del Caro, Cambridge University Press, Cambridge.
[3] 2007, *The Anti-Christ, Ecce Homo, The Twilight of the Idols, and Other Writing*, Arrows and Epigrams, 14, edited by Aaron Ridley and Judith Norman, translated by Judith Norman, (First published 2005), Cambridge University Press, Cambridge.

[4] 2012, *Nietzsche's Notebooks in English*: a Translator's Introduction and Afterward", [15 = WII 6a. Spring 1888], 15 [98], How to become a stronger, Translator Daniel Fidel Ferrer, USA.

[5] 1924, *The Complete Works of Friedrich Nietzsche, Volume Ten*, Book Third, 185, Poor, edited by Dr Oscar Levy, translated by Thomas Common, With Poetry Rendered by Paul V. Cohen and Maude D. Petre, The Macmillan Company, New York.

[6] 2006, Notebook 15, spring 1888, 15 [51], edited by Rüdiger Bittner, translated by Kate Sturge, (First published 2003), Cambridge University Press, Cambridge.

[7] 2006, Third Part, On Old and new Tablets, 12, edited by Adrian Del Caro and Robert Pippin, translated by Adrian Del Caro, Cambridge University Press, New York.

[8] 2006, Notebook 15, spring 1888, 15 [90], edited by Rüdiger Bittner, translated by Kate Sturge, (First published 2003), Cambridge University Press, Cambridge.

[9] 1989, Part Four, Epigrams and Interludes, 138, translated, with Commentary, by Walter Kaufmann, Vintage Books, A division of Random House, Inc., New York.

[10] 2006, First Part, The Speeches of Zarathustra, On The New Idol, edited by Adrian Del Caro and Robert Pippin, translated by Adrian Del Caro, Cambridge University Press, New York.

[11] 1967, Part One, Zarathustra's Discourses, Of the Tree on the Mountainside, translated by R.J. Hollingdale, Penguin Books, Baltimore, Maryland.

[12] 2006, Third Part, On Old and new Tablets, 7, edited by Adrian Del Caro and Robert Pippin, translated by Adrian Del Caro, Cambridge University Press, New York.

[13] 1989, Part One, On the Prejudices of Philosophers, 1, translated, with Commentary, by Walter Kaufmann, Vintage Books, A division of Random House, Inc., New York.

[14] 2012, *Nietzsche's Notebooks in English*: a Translator's Introduction and Afterward", [14 = WII 5. Spring 1888], 14 [173], Translator Daniel Fidel Ferrer, USA.

[15] 2012, *Nietzsche's Notebooks in English*: a Translator's Introduction and Afterward", [14 = WII 5. Spring 1888], 14 [159], Translator Daniel Fidel Ferrer, USA.

[16] 1924, *The Complete Works of Friedrich Nietzsche, Volume Ten*, Book Third, 175, Concerning Eloquence, edited by Dr Oscar Levy, translated by Thomas Common, With Poetry Rendered by Paul V. Cohen and Maude D. Petre, The Macmillan Company, New York.

[17] 2012, *Nietzsche's Notebooks in English*: a Translator's Introduction and Afterward", [15 = WII 6a. Spring 1888], 15 [6], 1, Translator Daniel Fidel Ferrer, USA.

[18] 1974, Book Three, 25, Spirit and character, translated, with commentary, by Walter Kaufmann, Vintage Books, New York.

[19] 1911, Part II, Part I. Miscellaneous Maxims and Opinions, 20, Truth Will Have No Gods Before It, translated by Paul V. Cohen, B.A., The Macmillan Company, New York.

[20] 1911, Part II, Part I. Miscellaneous Maxims and Opinions, 200, Original, translated by Paul V. Cohen, B.A., The Macmillan Company, New York.

[21] 1924, *The Complete Works of Friedrich Nietzsche, Volume Ten*, Book Third, 245, Praise in Choice, edited by Dr Oscar Levy, translated by Thomas Common, With Poetry Rendered by Paul V. Cohen and Maude D. Petre, The Macmillan Company, New York.

[22] 1996, Volume I, 2, On The History of the Moral Sentiments, 85, Wickedness is rare, translated by R.J. Hollingdale, Cambridge University Press, Cambridge.

[23] 1924, *The Complete Works of Friedrich Nietzsche, Volume Ten*, Book Third, 253, Always at Home, edited by Dr Oscar Levy, translated by Thomas Common, With Poetry Rendered by Paul V. Cohen and Maude D. Petre, The Macmillan Company, New York.

[24] 2002, Part 4, Epigrams and entr'actes, 160, ed. By Rolf-Peter Horstmann and Judith Norman, translated by Judith Norman, Cambridge University Press, New York.

[25] 1897, First Essay, "Good and Evil," "Good and Bad", 13, edited by Alexander Tille, translated by William A. Hauseman, Poems translated by John Gray, The Macmillan Company, London.

[26] 2006, First Part, The Speeches of Zarathustra, On the Flies of the Market Place, edited by Adrian Del Caro and Robert Pippin, translated by Adrian Del Caro, Cambridge University Press, New York.

[27] 1915, Part I, Fifth Division: The Signs of Higher and Lower Culture, 292, Forwards, translated by Helen Zimmern, The Macmillan Company, New York.

[28] 1990, History in the Service and Disservice of Life, Foreword, 4, translation by Gary Brown, William Arrowsmith, General Editor, Yale University Press, New Haven & London.

[29] 1996, Volume I, 9, Man Alone with Himself, 570, Shadow in the flame, translated by R.J. Hollingdale, Cambridge University Press, Cambridge.

[30] 1899, The First Part, Zarathustra's Speeches, Of Reading and Writing, translated by Alexander Tille, T. Fisher Unwin, London.

[31] 1899, The First Part, Zarathustra's Speeches, Of The Tree at The Hill, translated by Alexander Tille, T. Fisher Unwin, London.

[32] 1924, *The Complete Works of Friedrich Nietzsche, Volume Ten*, Book Third, 126, Mystical Explanations, edited by Dr Oscar Levy, translated by Thomas Common, With Poetry Rendered by Paul V. Cohen and Maude D. Petre, The Macmillan Company, New York.

[33] 1924, *The Complete Works of Friedrich Nietzsche, Volume Ten*, Book First, 52, What others Know of us, edited by Dr Oscar Levy, translated by Thomas Common, With Poetry Rendered by Paul V. Cohen and Maude D. Petre, The Macmillan Company, New York.

[34] 1974, Book Two, 76, The greatest Danger, translated, with commentary, by Walter Kaufmann, Vintage Books, New York.

[35] 2008, Book Three, 272, edited by Bernard Williams, translated by Josefine Nauckhoff, Poems translated by Adrian Del Caro, Cambridge University Press, Cambridge.

[36] 2006, Second Part, On the Pitying, edited by Adrian Del Caro and Robert Pippin, translated by Adrian Del Caro, Cambridge University Press, New York.

[37] 1911, Part II, Part I, Miscellaneous Maxims and Opinions, 368, Obscuring Oneself, translated by Paul V. Cohen, B.A., The Macmillan Company, New York.

[38] 2012, *Nietzsche's Notebooks in English*: a Translator's Introduction and Afterward", [20 = W II 10a. Summer 1888], 20 [69], Translator Daniel Fidel Ferrer, USA.

[39] 1974, "Joke, Cunning, and Revenge" Prelude in German Rhymes, 12, To a Light-

Lover, translated, with commentary, by Walter Kaufmann, Vintage Books, New York.

[40] 1911, Volume Two, Part One, Assorted Opinions and Maxims, 253, Impoliteness, translated by R.J. Hollingdale, Cambridge University Press, Cambridge.

[41] 2006, Second Part, On the Pitying, edited by Adrian Del Caro and Robert Pippin, translated by Adrian Del Caro, Cambridge University Press, New York.

[42] 1911, Part II, Part I, Miscellaneous Maxims and Opinions, 250, Reason for Dislike, translated by Paul V. Cohen, B.A., The Macmillan Company, New York.

[43] 1924, *The Complete Works of Friedrich Nietzsche, Volume Ten*, Book Third, 274, edited by Dr Oscar Levy, translated by Thomas Common, With Poetry Rendered by Paul V. Cohen and Maude D. Petre, The Macmillan Company, New York.

[44] 1911, Part II, Part II, The Wanderer and His Shadow, 288, How Far Machinery Humiliates, translated by Paul V. Cohen, B.A., The Macmillan Company, New York.

[45] 1911, Part II, Part II, The Wanderer and His Shadow, 306, Losing Ourselves, translated by Paul V. Cohen, B.A., The Macmillan Company, New York.

[46] 2007, *The Anti-Christ, Ecce Homo, The Twilight of the Idols, and Other Writing*, 52, edited by Aaron Ridley and Judith Norman, translated by Judith Norman, (First published 2005), Cambridge University Press, Cambridge.

[47] 1911, Part II, Part II, The Wanderer and His Shadow, 244, The Fox of foxes, translated by Paul V. Cohen, B.A., The Macmillan Company, New York.

[48] 1924, *The Complete Works of Friedrich Nietzsche, Volume Ten*, Book Third, 204, Beggars and Courtesy, edited by Dr Oscar Levy, translated by Thomas Common, With Poetry Rendered by Paul V. Cohen and Maude D. Petre, The Macmillan Company, New York.

[49] 1911, Part II, Part II, The Wanderer and His Shadow, 56, Intellect and Boredom, translated by Paul V. Cohen, B.A., The Macmillan Company, New York.

[50] 1924, *The Complete Works of Friedrich Nietzsche, Volume Ten*, Book Third, 242, Suumcuique, edited by Dr Oscar Levy, translated by Thomas Common, With Poetry rendered by Paul V. Cohen and Maude D. Petre, The Macmillan Company, New York.

[51] 1996, Volume I, 4, From The Soul of Artists and Writers, 192, The best author, translated by R.J. Hollingdale, Cambridge University Press, Cambridge.

[52] 2005, Book I, 48, Know yourself is the whole of science, edited by Maudemarie Clark and Brain Leiter, translated by R.J. Hollingrade, Cambridge University Press, Cambridge.

[53] 1915, Part I, Ninth Division: Man Alone by Himself, 547, The "Witty", translated by Helen Zimmern, The Macmillan Company, New York.

[54] 1924, *The Complete Works of Friedrich Nietzsche, Volume Ten*, Book Third, 201, edited by Dr Oscar Levy, translated by Thomas Common, With Poetry Rendered by Paul V. Cohen and Maude D. Petre, The Macmillan Company, New York.

[55] 2012, *Nietzsche's Notebooks in English*: a Translator's Introduction and Afterward", [20 = W II 10a. Summer 1888], 20 [20], Translator Daniel Fidel Ferrer, USA.

[56] 1924, *The Complete Works of Friedrich Nietzsche, Volume Ten*, Book Third, 275, edited by Dr Oscar Levy, translated by Thomas Common, With Poetry Rendered by Paul V. Cohen and Maude D. Petre, The Macmillan Company, New York.

[57] 2012, *Nietzsche's Notebooks in English*: a Translator's Introduction and Afterward",

[20 = W II 10a. Summer 1888], 20 [130], Translator Daniel Fidel Ferrer, USA.

[58] 1899, The First Part, Zarathustra's Speeches, Of Reading and Writing, translated by Alexander Tille, T. Fisher Unwin, London.

[59] 1924, *The Complete Works of Friedrich Nietzsche, Volume Ten*, Book Third, 263, edited by Dr Oscar Levy, translated by Thomas Common, With Poetry Rendered by Paul V. Cohen and Maude D. Petre, The Macmillan Company, New York.

[60] 2012, *Nietzsche's Notebooks in English*: a Translator's Introduction and Afterward", [20 = W II 10a. Summer 1888], 20 [43], Translator Daniel Fidel Ferrer, USA.

[61] 1911, Part II, Part I, The Wanderer and His Shadow, 298, From The Practice of the Wise, translated by Paul V. Cohen, B.A., The Macmillan Company, New York.

[62] 1899, The First Part, Zarathustra's Speeches, Of The Tree at The Hill, translated by Alexander Tille, T. Fisher Unwin, London.

[63] 2012, *Nietzsche's Notebooks in English*: a Translator's Introduction and Afterward", [20 = W II 10a. Summer 1888], 20 [46], Translator Daniel Fidel Ferrer, USA.

[64] 1924, *The Complete Works of Friedrich Nietzsche, Volume Ten*, Book Fifth, We Fearless Ones, 344, To what Extent Even We are still Pious, edited by Dr Oscar Levy, translated by Thomas Common, With Poetry Rendered by Paul V. Cohen and Maude D. Petre, The Macmillan Company, New York.

[65] 2012, *Nietzsche's Notebooks in English*: a Translator's Introduction and Afterward", [14 = WII 5. Spring 1888], 14 [80], Translator Daniel Fidel Ferrer, USA.

[66] 1989, Part Four, Epigrams and Interludes, 158, translated, with Commentary, by Walter Kaufmann, Vintage Books, A division of Random House, Inc., New York.

[67] 1899, Zarathustra's Introductory Speech On Beyond-Man and The Last Man, 10, translated by Alexander Tille, T. Fisher Unwin, London.

[68] 1974, Book Four, Sanctus Januarius, 334, One must learn to Love, translated, with commentary, by Walter Kaufmann, Vintage Books, New York.

[69] 1989, Part Two, The Free Spirit, 24, translated, with Commentary, by Walter Kaufmann, Vintage Books, A division of Random House, Inc., New York.

[70] 2008, Book Three, 247, Habit, edited by Bernard Williams, translated by Josefine Nauckhoff, Poems translated by Adrian Del Caro, Cambridge University Press, Cambridge.

[71] 1996, Volume I, 4, From The Soul of Artists and Writers, 188 Thinkers as stylists, translated by R.J. Hollingdale, Cambridge University Press, Cambridge.

[72] 1996, Volume I, 2, On The History of the Moral Sentiments, 83 Sleep of virtue, translated by R.J. Hollingdale, Cambridge University Press, Cambridge.

[73] 2012, *Nietzsche's Notebooks in English*: a Translator's Introduction and Afterward", [16 = WII 7a. Spring-Summer 1888], 16 [40], 2, Translator Daniel Fidel Ferrer, USA.

[74] 2012, *Nietzsche's Notebooks in English*: a Translator's Introduction and Afterward", [20 = W II 10a. Summer 1888], 20 [90], Translator Daniel Fidel Ferrer, USA.

[75] 1996, Volume I, 4, From The Soul of Artists and Writers, 186 Wit, translated by R.J. Hollingdale, Cambridge University Press, Cambridge.

Notes of the Chapter II:

[1] 2012, *Nietzsche's Notebooks in English*: a Translator's Introduction and Afterward,

[20 = W II 10a. Summer 1888], 20 [70], Translator Daniel Fidel Ferrer, USA.

[2] 1911, Part II, Part II. The Wanderer and His Shadow, 18, The Moder Diogenes, translated by Paul V. Cohen, B.A., The Macmillan Company, New York.

[3] 2005, Book III, 180, Wars, edited by Maudemarie Clark and Brain Leiter, translated by R.J. Hollingrade, Cambridge University Press, Cambridge.

[4] 1909, Fourth Chapter, Apophthegms and Interludes, 73 A, edited by Dr Oscar Levy, v.5., translated by Helen Zimmern, T.N. Foulis, Edinburgh and London.

[5] 1911, Part II, Part I. Miscellaneous Maxims and Opinions, 246, The Sage Giving Himself Out to Be a Fool, translated by Paul V. Cohen, B.A., The Macmillan Company, New York.

[6] 1967, Part Three, Zarathustra's Discourses, Of Old and New Law-Tables, 20, translated by R.J. Hollingdale, Penguin Books, Baltimore, Maryland.

[7] 1915, Part I, Sixth Division: Man in Society, 317, Motive of an Attack, translated by Helen Zimmern, The Macmillan Company, New York.

[8] 2006, Notebook 5, summer 1886 – autumn 1887, 6, edited by Rüdiger Bittner, translated by Kate Strurge, (First published 2003), Cambridge University Press, Cambridge.

[9] 1911, *The Complete Works of Friedrich Nietzsche, Volume Seventeen*, Why I Am a Fatality, 1, edited by Dr. Oscar Levy, translated by Anthony M. Ludovici, Poetry Rendered by: Paul V. Cohen, Herman Scheffauer, Francis Bickley, Dr. G.T. Wrench, The Macmillan Company, New York.

[10] 2007, *The Anti-Christ, Ecce Homo, The Twilight of the Idols, and Other Writing*, Skirmishes of an Untimely Man, 39, Critique of modernity, edited by Aaron Ridley and Judith Norman, translated by Judith Norman, (First published 2005), Cambridge University Press, Cambridge.

[11] 1899, *The Case of Wagner, Nietzsche contra Wagner, The Twilight of the Idols, The Antichrist*, Apophthegms and Darts, 4, translated by Thomas Common, T. Fisher Unwin, London.

[12] 1911, Part II, Part II, The Wanderer and His Shadow, 254, To The Light, translated by Paul V. Cohen, B.A., The Macmillan Company, New York.

[13] 2012, *Nietzsche's Notebooks in English*: a Translator's Introduction and Afterward, [20 = W II 10a. Summer 1888], 20 [67], Translator Daniel Fidel Ferrer, USA.

[14] 1967, Part One, Zarathustra's Discourses, Of Chastity, translated by R.J. Hollingdale, Penguin Books, Baltimore, Maryland.

[15] 2012, *Nietzsche's Notebooks in English*: a Translator's Introduction and Afterward, [20 = W II 10a. Summer 1888], 20 [151], Translator Daniel Fidel Ferrer, USA.

[16] 1911, Part II, Part I, Miscellaneous Maxims and Opinions, 164, In Favour of Critics, translated by Paul V. Cohen, B.A., The Macmillan Company, New York.

[17] 1917, First Part, Neighbour-Love, translated by Thomas Common, the Modern Library, New York.

[18] 1967, Part Three, Zarathustra's Discourses, The Second Dancing Song, 1, translated by R.J. Hollingdale, Penguin Books, Baltimore, Maryland.

[19] 1967, Part One, Zarathustra's Prologue, 7, translated by R.J. Hollingdale, Penguin Books, Baltimore, Maryland.

[20] 1911, Part II, Part I, Miscellaneous Maxims and Opinions, 346, Being misunder-

stood, translated by Paul V. Cohen, B.A., The Macmillan Company, New York.

[21] 2005, Book IV, 313, The friend whom we want no longer, edited by Maudemarie Clark and Brain Leiter, translated by R.J. Hollingrade, Cambridge University Press, Cambridge.

[22] 1899, The First Part, Zarathustra's Speeches, Of The New Idol, translated by Alexander Tille, T. Fisher Unwin, London.

[23] 2006, Fourth and Final Part, On the Higher Man, 15, edited by Adrian Del Caro and Robert Pippin, translated by Adrian Del Caro, Cambridge University Press, New York.

[24] 1911, Volume Two, Part One, Assorted Opinions and Maxims, 386, A Defective Ear, translated by R.J. Hollingdale, Cambridge University Press, Cambridge.

[25] 2006, Fourth and Final Part, On the Higher Man, 12, edited by Adrian Del Caro and Robert Pippin, translated by Adrian Del Caro, Cambridge University Press, New York.

[26] 2006, Third Part, Before Sunrise, edited by Adrian Del Caro and Robert Pippin, translated by Adrian Del Caro, Cambridge University Press, New York.

[27] 1911, Part II, Part II, The Wanderer and His Shadow, 38, The Sting of Conscience, translated by Paul V. Cohen, B.A., The Macmillan Company, New York.

[28] 1899, The First Part, Zarathustra's Speeches, Of Reading and Writing, translated by Alexander Tille, T. Fisher Unwin, London.

[29] 1915, Part I, Ninth Division: Man Alone by Himself, 579, Unsuitable for A Party-Man, translated by Helen Zimmern, The Macmillan Company, New York.

[30] 1967, Part Three, Zarathustra's Discourses, Of Old and New Law-Tables, 20, translated by R.J. Hollingdale, Penguin Books, Baltimore, Maryland.

[31] 1967, Part Four, Zarathustra's Discourses, Of the Higher Man, 14, translated by R.J. Hollingdale, Penguin Books, Baltimore, Maryland.

[32] 2011, The Complete Works of Friedrich Nietzsche, Volume Five, Book Two, 112, On the natural history of duty and right, translated by Brittain Smith, Afterword by Keith Ansell-Pearson, Stanford University Press, Stanford, California.

[33] 1909, Second Chapter, The Free Spirit, 34, edited by Dr Oscar Levy, v.5., translated by Helen Zimmern, T.N. Foulis, Edinburgh and London.

[34] 1899, The First Part, Zarathustra's Speeches, Of A Thousand and One Goals, translated by Alexander Tille, T. Fisher Unwin, London.

[35] 1915, Part I, Ninth Division: Man Alone by Himself, 536, The Value of Insipid Opponents, translated by Helen Zimmern, The Macmillan Company, New York.

[36] 1899, The First Part, Zarathustra's Speeches, Of Free Death, translated by Alexander Tille, T. Fisher Unwin, London.

[37] 1974, Joke, Cunning, and Revenge, 32, The Unfree Man, translated, with commentary, by Walter Kaufmann, Vintage Books, New York.

[38] 1915, Part I, Fifth Division: The Signs of Higher and Lower Culture, 283, The Chief Deficiency Of Active People, translated by Helen Zimmern, The Macmillan Company, New York.

[39] 1917, Second Part, The Sublime Ones, translated by Thomas Common, the Modern Library, New York.

[40] 1917, First Part, The Bite of the Adder, translated by Thomas Common, the

Modern Library, New York.

[41] 1996, Volume I, 9, Man Alone with Himself, 529, The length of the day, translated by R.J. Hollingdale, Cambridge University Press, Cambridge.

[42] 1924, T*he Complete Works of Friedrich Nietzsche, Volume Ten*, Book Third, 179, Thoughts, edited by Dr Oscar Levy, translated by Thomas Common, With Poetry Rendered by Paul V. Cohen and Maude D. Petre, The Macmillan Company, New York.

[43] 1996, Volume I, 1, Of First and Last Things, 33, Error regarding life necessary to life, translated by R.J. Hollingdale, Cambridge University Press, Cambridge.

[44] 1924, *The Complete Works of Friedrich Nietzsche, Volume Ten*, Book Fourth, Sanctus Januaris, 290, One Thing is Needful, edited by Dr Oscar Levy, translated by Thomas Common, With Poetry Rendered by Paul V. Cohen and Maude D. Petre, The Macmillan Company, New York.

[45] 1917, Third Part, Old and New Tables, 14, translated by Thomas Common, the Modern Library, New York.

[46] 1924, *The Complete Works of Friedrich Nietzsche, Volume Ten*, Book Third, 219, The Object of Punishment, edited by Dr Oscar Levy, translated by Thomas Common, With Poetry Rendered by Paul V. Cohen and Maude D. Petre, The Macmillan Company, New York.

[47] 1917, Third Part, The Wanderer, translated by Thomas Common, the Modern Library, New York.

[48] 1915, Part I, Second Division: The History of The Moral Sentiments, 39, The Fable Of Intelligible Freedom, translated by Helen Zimmern, The Macmillan Company, New York.

[49] 1915, Part I, Third Division: The Religious Life, 118, Change of Front, translated by Helen Zimmern, The Macmillan Company, New York.

[50] 1899, The Second Part, Of Tarantulae, translated by Alexander Tille, T. Fisher Unwin, London.

[51] 1924, *The Complete Works of Friedrich Nietzsche, Volume Ten*, Book Third, 223, Vicariousness of the Senses, edited by Dr Oscar Levy, translated by Thomas Common, With Poetry Rendered by Paul V. Cohen and Maude D. Petre, The Macmillan Company, New York.

[52] 1924, *The Complete Works of Friedrich Nietzsche, Volume Ten*, Book Third, 222, Poet and Liar, edited by Dr Oscar Levy, translated by Thomas Common, With Poetry Rendered by Paul V. Cohen and Maude D. Petre, The Macmillan Company, New York.

[53] 2012, *Nietzsche's Notebooks in English*: a Translator's Introduction and Afterward, [20 = W II 10a. Summer 1888], 20 [24], Translator Daniel Fidel Ferrer, USA.

[54] 1974, Book Three, 229, Obstinacy and faithfulness, translated, with commentary, by Walter Kaufmann, Vintage Books, New York.

[55] 1899, The First Part, Zarathustra's Speeches, Of Poets, translated by Alexander Tille, T. Fisher Unwin, London.

[56] 1924, *The Complete Works of Friedrich Nietzsche, Volume Ten*, Book Third, 195, Laughable!, edited by Dr Oscar Levy, translated by Thomas Common, With Poetry Rendered by Paul V. Cohen and Maude D. Petre, The Macmillan Company, New York.

[57] 1899, The Third Part, On The Mount of Olives, translated by Alexander Tille, T. Fisher Unwin, London.

[58] 1911, Part II, Part I. Miscellaneous Maxims and Opinions, 48, The Possession of Joy Abounding, translated by Paul V. Cohen, B.A., The Macmillan Company, New York.

[59] 1899, Zarathustra's Introductory Speech on Beyond-Man and The Last Man, 5, translated by Alexander Tille, T. Fisher Unwin, London.

[60] 1924, *The Complete Works of Friedrich Nietzsche, Volume Ten*, Book First, 77, The Animal with good Conscience, edited by Dr Oscar Levy, translated by Thomas Common, With Poetry Rendered by Paul V. Cohen and Maude D. Petre, The Macmillan Company, New York.

[61] 1911, Part II, Part II, The Wanderer and His Shadow, 324, Becoming a Thinker, translated by Paul V. Cohen, B.A., The Macmillan Company, New York.

1911, Part II, Part II, The Wanderer and His Shadow, 324, Becoming a Thinker, translated by Paul V. Cohen, B.A., The Macmillan Company, New York.

[62] 1924, *The Complete Works of Friedrich Nietzsche, Volume Ten*, Book Third, 160, Too Jewish, edited by Dr Oscar Levy, translated by Thomas Common, With Poetry Rendered by Paul V. Cohen and Maude D. Petre, The Macmillan Company, New York.

[63] 1913, Third Essay, What Is the Meaning of Ascetic Ideals, 8, translated by Horace B. Samuel, M.A., T.N. Foulis, Edinburgh and London.

[64] 1899, The First Part, Zarathustra's Speeches, Of The Despisers of Body, translated by Alexander Tille, T. Fisher Unwin, London.

[65] 1911, Part II, Part II, The Wanderer and His Shadow, 13, Repetition, translated by Paul V. Cohen, B.A., The Macmillan Company, New York.

[66] 1899, The First Part, Zarathustra's Speeches, Of Delights and Passions, translated by Alexander Tille, T. Fisher Unwin, London.

[67] 1915, Part I, Ninth Division: Man Alone by Himself, 519, Truth as Circe, translated by Helen Zimmern, The Macmillan Company, New York.

[68] 1915, Part I, Ninth Division: Man Alone by Himself, 531, The Enemy's Life, translated by Helen Zimmern, The Macmillan Company, New York

[69] 1924, *The Complete Works of Friedrich Nietzsche, Volume Ten*, Book Fifth, We Fearless Ones, 380, "The Wanderer" Speaks, edited by Dr Oscar Levy, translated by Thomas Common, With Poetry rendered by Paul V. Cohen and Maude D. Petre, The Macmillan Company, New York.

[70] 1915, Part I, Ninth Division: Man Alone by Himself, 541, In The Current, translated by Helen Zimmern, The Macmillan Company, New York.

[71] 1924, *The Complete Works of Friedrich Nietzsche, Volume Ten*, Book Fourth, Sanctus Januaris, 312, My Dog, edited by Dr Oscar Levy, translated by Thomas Common, With Poetry Rendered by Paul V. Cohen and Maude D. Petre, The Macmillan Company, New York.

[72] 2012, *Nietzsche's Notebooks in English*: a Translator's Introduction and Afterward, [20 = W II 10a. Summer 1888], 20 [29], Translator Daniel Fidel Ferrer, USA.

[73] 1915, Part I, Ninth Division: Man Alone by Himself, 527 Sticking to an Opinion, translated by Helen Zimmern, The Macmillan Company, New York.

[74] 1899, The First Part, Zarathustra's Speeches, Of Reading and Writing, translated by

Alexander Tille, T. Fisher Unwin, London.

[75] 1915, Part I, Ninth Division: Man Alone by Himself, 499, Friends, translated by Helen Zimmern, The Macmillan Company, New York.

Notes of the Chapter III:

[1] 1989, Part Four, Epigrams and Interludes, 153, translated, with Commentary, by Walter Kaufmann, Vintage Books, A division of Random House, Inc., New York.

[2] 2012, *Nietzsche's Notebooks in English*: a translator's Introduction and Afterward, [20 = W II 10a. Summer 1888], 20 [62], Translator Daniel Fidel Ferrer, USA.

[3] 1999, Fourth and last part, LXII The Cry of Distress, translated by Thomas Common, Dover Publications, Inc. Mineola, New York.

[4] 2005, Book III, 185, Beggars, edited by Maudemarie Clark and Brain Leiter, translated by R.J. Hollingrade, Cambridge University Press, Cambridge.

[5] 1899, The First Part, Zarathustra's Speeches, Of The Way of A Creator, translated by Alexander Tille, T. Fisher Unwin, London.

[6] 2012, *Nietzsche's Notebooks in English*: a Translator's Introduction and Afterward, [20 = W II 10a. Summer 1888], 20 [124], Translator Daniel Fidel Ferrer, USA.

[7] 2010, Introduction, I, Reading strategies, from a notebook from 1881-2, edited by Raymond Geuss; Alexander Nehamas, translated by Ladislaus Löb, (First published 2009), Cambridge University Press, Cambridge.

[8] 1911, Part II, Part I, Miscellaneous Maxims and Opinions, 53, Envy with or without a Mouthpiece, translated by Paul V. Cohen, B.A., The Macmillan Company, New York.

[9] 2007, Why I Write Such Good Books, Thus Spoke Zarathustra, A Book for Everyone and Nobody, 8, translated with an Introduction and Notes by Duncan Large, Oxford University Press, New York.

[10] 1989, Why I Am So Wise, 2, translated by Walter Kaufmann, edited, with commentary by Walter Kaufmann, Vintage Books, New York.

[11] 1911, Part II, Part I, Miscellaneous Maxims and Opinions, 232, THE PROFOUND, translated by Paul V. Cohen, B.A., The Macmillan Company, New York.

[12] 1899, The First Part, Zarathustra's Speeches, Of Reading and Writing, translated by Alexander Tille, T. Fisher Unwin, London.

[13] 1967, Part One, Zarathustra's Discourses, Of Love of One's Neighbour, translated by R.J. Hollingdale, Penguin Books, Baltimore, Maryland.

[14] 1989, Part Four, Epigrams and Interludes, 180, translated, with Commentary, by Walter Kaufmann, Vintage Books, A division of Random House, Inc., New York.

[15] 2006, Notebook 14, spring 1888, 14 [174], Edited by Rüdiger Bittner, translated by Kate Strurge, (First published 2003), Cambridge University Press, Cambridge.

[16] 1899, *The Case of Wagner, Nietzsche contra Wagner, The Twilight of the Idols, The Antichrist*, Apophthegms and Darts, 5, translated by Thomas Common, T. Fisher Unwin, London.

[17] 2007, *The Anti-Christ, Ecce Homo, The Twilight of the Idols, and Other Writing*, Arrows and Epigrams, 37, Edited by Aaron Ridley and Judith Norman, translated by Judith Norman, (First published 2005), Cambridge University Press, Cambridge.

[18] 2006, Notebook 14, spring 1888, 14[148], Edited by Rüdiger Bittner, translated by Kate Strurge, (First published 2003), Cambridge University Press, Cambridge.

[19] 2007, *The Anti-Christ, Ecce Homo, The Twilight of the Idols, and Other Writing*, Arrows and Epigrams, 17, edited by Aaron Ridley and Judith Norman, translated by Judith Norman, (First published 2005), Cambridge University Press, Cambridge.

[20] 1899, The First Part, Zarathustra's Speeches, Of The Chairs of Virtue, translated by Alexander Tille, T. Fisher Unwin, London.

[21] 2007, *The Anti-Christ, Ecce Homo, The Twilight of the Idols, and Other Writing*, "Improveing" Humanity, 1, edited by Aaron Ridley and Judith Norman, translated by Judith Norman, (First published 2005), Cambridge University Press, Cambridge.

[22] 2006, Notebook 2, autumn 1885 – autumn 1886, 2 [112], Edited by Rüdiger Bittner, translated by Kate Strurge, (First published 2003), Cambridge University Press, Cambridge.

[23] 1999, First Part, IV The Despisers of the Body, translated by Thomas Common, Dover Publications, Inc. Mineola, New York.

[24] 2007, 1, *The Anti-Christ, Ecce Homo, The Twilight of the Idols, and Other Writing*, edited by Aaron Ridley and Judith Norman, translated by Judith Norman, (First published 2005), Cambridge University Press, Cambridge.

[25] 1899, The First Part, Zarathustra's Speeches, Of The Tree at The Hill, translated by Alexander Tille, T. Fisher Unwin, London.

[26] 1999, Third Part, LVI Old and New Tables, 13, translated by Thomas Common, Dover Publications, Inc. Mineola, New York.

[27] 1911, *The Complete Works of Friedrich Nietzsche, Volume Nine*, Book V, 573, Casting One's Skin, edited by Dr. Oscar Levy, Translated by J. M. Kennedy, The Macmillan Company, New York.

[28] 1911, Part II, Part I, Miscellaneous Maxims and Opinions, 122, Good Memory, translated by Paul V. Cohen, B.A., The Macmillan Company, New York.

[29] 1924, *The Complete Works of Friedrich Nietzsche, Volume Ten*, Book First, 7, Something for the Laborious, edited by Dr Oscar Levy, translated by Thomas Common, With Poetry Rendered by Paul V. Cohen and Maude D. Petre, The Macmillan Company, New York.

[30] 1917, Third Part, The Bedwarfing Virtue, 3, translated by Thomas Common, the Modern Library, New York.

[31] 1917, Third Part, The Spirit of Gravity, 2, translated by Thomas Common, the Modern Library, New York.

[32] 2005, Book III, 200, Enduring poverty, edited by Maudemarie Clark and Brain Leiter, translated by R.J. Hollingrade, Cambridge University Press, Cambridge.

[33] 2012, *Nietzsche's Notebooks in English*: a Translator's Introduction and Afterward, [20 = W II 10a. Summer 1888], 20 [11], Translator Daniel Fidel Ferrer, USA.

[34] 1989, Why I Write Such Good Books, The Untimely Ones, 2, translated by Walter Kaufmann, edited, with commentary by Walter Kaufmann, Vintage Books, New York.

[35] 1924, *The Complete Works of Friedrich Nietzsche, Volume Ten*, Book Third, 244, Thoughts and Words, edited by Dr Oscar Levy, translated by Thomas Common, With Poetry Rendered by Paul V. Cohen and Maude D. Petre, The Macmillan Company, New York.

[36] 2012, *Nietzsche's Notebooks in English*: a Translator's Introduction and Afterward, [20 = W II 10a. Summer 1888], 20 [78], Translator Daniel Fidel Ferrer, USA.

[37] 1915, Part I, Ninth Division: Man Alone by Himself, 568, Confession, translated by Helen Zimmern, The Macmillan Company, New York.

[38] 2006, Third Part, The Convalescent, 1, edited by Adrian Del Caro and Robert Pippin, translated by Adrian Del Caro, Cambridge University Press, New York.

[39] 1899, The First Part, Zarathustra's Speeches, Of A Thousand and One Goals, translated by Alexander Tille, T. Fisher Unwin, London.

[40] 1967, Part Four, Zarathustra's Discourses, The Intoxicated Song, 10, translated by R.J. Hollingdale, Penguin Books, Baltimore, Maryland.

[41] 1915, Part I, Ninth Division: Man Alone by Himself, 536, The Value Of Insipid Opponents, translated by Helen Zimmern, The Macmillan Company, New York.

[42] 1924, *The Complete Works of Friedrich Nietzsche, Volume Ten*, Book Third, 257, From Experience, edited by Dr Oscar Levy, translated by Thomas Common, With Poetry Rendered by Paul V. Cohen and Maude D. Petre, The Macmillan Company, New York.

[43] 2008, Appendix: Songs of Prince Vogelfrei, Rimus Remedium, or: How sick poets console themselves, edited by Bernard Williams, translated by Josefine Nauckhoff, Poems translated by Adrian Del Caro, Cambridge University Press, Cambridge University.

[44] 2007, *The Anti-Christ, Ecce Homo, The Twilight of the Idols, and Other Writing*, 57, edited by Aaron Ridley and Judith Norman, translated by Judith Norman, (First published 2005), Cambridge University Press, Cambridge.

[45] 1911, *The Complete Works of Friedrich Nietzsche, Volume Nine*, Book III, 178, Daily Wear and Tear, edited by Dr. Oscar Levy, translated by J. M. Kennedy, The Macmillan Company, New York.

[46] 2006, Third Part, The Other Dance Song, 1, edited by Adrian Del Caro and Robert Pippin, translated by Adrian Del Caro, Cambridge University Press, New York.

[47] 1999, The Birth of Tragedy out of the Spirit of Music, 24, edited by Raymond Geuss and Ronald Speirs, translated by Ronald Speirs, Cambridge University Press, Cambridge.

[48] 2008, Book Three, 272, edited by Bernard Williams, translated by Josefine Nauckhoff, Poems translated by Adrian Del Caro, Cambridge University Press, Cambridge University.

[49] 2011, *The Complete Works of Friedrich Nietzsche, Volume Five*, Book Four, 252, Consider!, translated by Brittain Smith, Afterword by Keith Ansell-Pearson, Stanford University Press, Stanford, California.

[50] 2006, First Part, The Speeches of Zarathustra, On the Bestowing Virtue, 3, edited by Adrian Del Caro and Robert Pippin, translated by Adrian Del Caro, Cambridge University Press, New York.

[51] 1915, Part I, Ninth Division: Man Alone by Himself, 580, A Bad Memory, translated by Helen Zimmern, The Macmillan Company, New York.

[52] 1915, Part I, Seventh Division: Wife and Child, 381, Correcting Nature, translated by Helen Zimmern, The Macmillan Company, New York.

[53] 1915, Part I, Ninth Division: Man Alone by Himself, 485, Decided Character,

translated by Helen Zimmern, The Macmillan Company, New York.

[54] 1924, *The Complete Works of Friedrich Nietzsche, Volume Ten*, Book Third, 222, Poet and Liar, edited by Dr Oscar Levy, translated by Thomas Common, With Poetry Rendered by Paul V. Cohen and Maude D. Petre, The Macmillan Company, New York.

[55] 1911, Part II, Part I. Miscellaneous Maxims and Opinions, 130, Readers Insults, translated by Paul V. Cohen, B.A., The Macmillan Company, New York.

[56] 1924, The Complete Works of Friedrich Nietzsche, Volume Ten, Book Third, 229, Obstinacy and Loyalty, edited by Dr Oscar Levy, translated by Thomas Common, With Poetry rendered by Paul V. Cohen and Maude D. Petre, The Macmillan Company, New York.

[57] 1899, The First Part, Zarathustra's Speeches, Of Reading and Writing, translated by Alexander Tille, T. Fisher Unwin, London.

[58] 1899, The First Part, Zarathustra's Speeches, Of The Chairs of Virtue, translated by Alexander Tille, T. Fisher Unwin, London.

[59] 1899, Zarathustra's Introductory Speech On Beyond-Man and The Last Man, 9, translated by Alexander Tille, T. Fisher Unwin, London.

[60] 1911, Part II, Part I, Miscellaneous Maxims and Opinions, 404, How Duty Acquires a Glamour, translated by Paul V. Cohen, B.A., The Macmillan Company, New York.

[61] 1911, Part II, Part I, Miscellaneous Maxims and Opinions, 160, Advantage for Opponents, translated by Paul V. Cohen, B.A., The Macmillan Company, New York.

62 2012, *Nietzsche's Notebooks in English*: a Translator's Introduction and Afterward, [20 = W II 10a. Summer 1888], 20 [82], Translator Daniel Fidel Ferrer, USA.

[63] 1899, Zarathustra's Introductory Speech On Beyond-Man and The Last Man, 4, translated by Alexander Tille, T. Fisher Unwin, London.

[64] 1911, Part II, Part II, The Wanderer and His Shadow, 347, Also Worthy of A Hero, translated by Paul V. Cohen, B.A., The Macmillan Company, New York.

[65] 1911, Part II, Part II, The Wanderer and His Shadow, 302, How We Seek to Improve Bad Arguments, translated by Paul V. Cohen, B.A., The Macmillan Company, New York.

[66] 1911, Part II, Part II, The Wanderer and His Shadow, 341, Wheel and Drag, translated by Paul V. Cohen, B.A., The Macmillan Company, New York.

[67] 1897, Second Essay, "Guilt," "Bad Conscience," And The Like, 6, edited by Alexander Tille, translated by William A. Hauseman, Poems translated by John Gray, The Macmillan Company, London.

[68] 1924, *The Complete Works of Friedrich Nietzsche, Volume Ten*, Book Third, 239, The Joyless Person, edited by Dr Oscar Levy, translated by Thomas Common, With Poetry Rendered by Paul V. Cohen and Maude D. Petre, The Macmillan Company, New York.

[69] 1915, Part I, Ninth Division: Man Alone by Himself, 502, The Unassuming Man, translated by Helen Zimmern, The Macmillan Company, New York.

[70] 1915, Part I, Ninth Division: Man Alone by Himself, 554, Partial Knowledge, translated by Helen Zimmern, The Macmillan Company, New York.

[71] 2012, *Nietzsche's Notebooks in English*: a Translator's Introduction and Afterward,

[20 = W II 10a. Summer 1888], 20 [22], Translator Daniel Fidel Ferrer, USA.
[72] 1911, *The case of Wagner; II. Nietzsche contra Wagner; III. Selected Aphorisms*, translated by Anthony M. Ludovici, (3d ed.), *IV. We philologists, The case of Wagner, Epilogue*, translated by J. M. Kennedy, T. N. Foulis, Edinburgh.
[73] 1924, The Complete Works of Friedrich Nietzsche, Volume Ten, Book Third, 269, edited by Dr Oscar Levy, translated by Thomas Common, With Poetry rendered by Paul V. Cohen and Maude D. Petre, The Macmillan Company, New York.
[74] 1915, Part I, Ninth Division: Man Alone by Himself, 516, Truth, translated by Helen Zimmern, The Macmillan Company, New York.
[75] 2008, "Joke, Cunning, and Revenge" Prelude in German Rhymes, 55, The Realistic Painter, edited by Bernard Williams, translated by Josefine Nauckhoff, Poems translated by Adrian Del Caro, Cambridge University Press, Cambridge University.

Notes of the End:
[1] 1924, *The Complete Works of Friedrich Nietzsche, Volume Ten*, Jest, Ruse and Revenge, 54, edited by Dr Oscar Levy, translated by Thomas Common, With Poetry Rendered by Paul V. Cohen and Maude D. Petre, The Macmillan Company, New York.
[2] 1899, The First Part, Zarathustra's Speeches, Of Reading and Writing, translated by Alexander Tille, T. Fisher Unwin, London.
[3] 1996, Volume One, Preface, 1, translated by R.J. Hollingdale, Cambridge University Press, Cambridge.
[4] 1899, *The Case of Wagner, Nietzsche contra Wagner, The Twilight of the Idols, The Antichrist*, Roving Expeditions of an Inopportune Philosopher, 51, translated by Thomas Common, T. Fisher Unwin, London.
[5] 2012, *Nietzsche's Notebooks in English*: a Translator's Introduction and Afterward", [21 = NVII 4. Autumn 1888], 21 [4], translator Daniel Fidel Ferrer, USA.
[6] 1899, Zarathustra's Introductory Speech On Beyond-Man and The Last Man, 5, translated by Alexander Tille, T. Fisher Unwin, London.
[7] 1897, Third Essay What Do Ascetic Ideals Mean? 7, edited by Alexander Tille, translated by William A. Hauseman, Poems Translated by John Gray, The Macmillan Company, London.
[8] 2012, *Nietzsche's Notebooks in English*: a Translator's Introduction and Afterward, [20 = W II 10a. Summer 1888], The brazen silence 20 [98], Translator Daniel Fidel Ferrer, USA.
[9] 1924, *The Complete Works of Friedrich Nietzsche, Volume Ten*, Book Third, New Struggles, 108, Edited by Dr Oscar Levy, translated by Thomas Common, With Poetry Rendered by Paul V. Cohen and Maude D. Petre, The Macmillan Company, New York.
[10] 1911, Part II, Part I. Miscellaneous Maxims and Opinions, 357, Disloyalty A Condition or Mastery, Translated by Paul V. Cohen, B.A., The Macmillan Company, New York.

Bibliography

The Birth of Tragedy
 Nietzsche, F. (1999). *The Birth of Tragedy And Other Writing*, Edited by Raymond Geuss and Ronald Speirs, Translated by Ronald Speirs, Cambridge University Press, Cambridge.

Unmodern Observations/Untimely Meditations
 Nietzsche, F. (2007). *Untimely Meditations*, Translated by R.J. Hollingrade, (First published 1997) Cambridge University Press, Cambridge.
 Nietzsche, F. (1990). *Unmodern Observations*, Translation by Gary Brown, William Arrowsmith, General Editor, YALE UNIVERSITY PRESS, New Haven & London.

Human, All Too Human
 Nietzsche, F. (1996). *Human, All Too Human*, Translated by R.J. Hollingdale, Cambridge University Press, Cambridge.
 Nietzsche, F. (1915). *Human, All Too Human*, Translated by Helen Zimmern, The Macmillan Company, New York.
 Nietzsche, F. (1911). *Human, All Too Human*, Translated by Paul V. Cohen, B.A., The Macmillan Company, New York.

Daybreak, Thoughts on the Prejudices of Morality/Dawn Thoughts on the Presumptions of Morality/The Dawn Of Day
 Nietzsche, F. (2011). *The Complete Works of Friedrich Nietzsche, Dawn Thoughts on the Presumptions of Morality*, Volume Five, Translated by Brittain Smith, Afterword by Keith Ansell-Pearson, Stanford University Press, Stanford, California.
 Nietzsche, F. (2005). *Daybreak, Thoughts on the Prejudices of Morality*, Edited by Maudemarie Clark and Brain Leiter, Translated by R.J. Hollingrade, Cambridge University Press, Cambridge (First Published 1997).
 Nietzsche, F. (1911). *The Complete Works of Friedrich Nietzsche, The Dawn Of Day*, Volume Nine, Book IV, 294, SAINTS, Edited by Dr. Oscar Levy, Translated by J. M. Kennedy, The Macmillan Company, New York .

The Gay Science/ The Joyful Wisdom
 Nietzsche, F. (2008). *The Gay Science*, Edited by Bernard Williams, Translated by Josefine Nauckhoff, Poems Translated by Adrian Del Caro, Cambridge University Press, Cambridge University.
 Nietzsche, F. (1974). *The Gay Science*, Translated, with commentary, by Walter Kaufmann, Vintage Books, New York.

Nietzsche, F. (1924). *The Joyful Wisdom, The Complete Works of Friedrich Nietzsche*, Volume Ten, Edited by Dr Oscar Levy, Translated by Thomas Common, With Poetry Rendered by Paul V. Cohen and Maude D. Petre, The Macmillan Company, New York.

Thus Spoke Zarathustra/Thus Spake Zarathustra
Nietzsche, F. (2006). *Thus Spoke Zarathustra*, edited by Adrian Del Caro and Robert Pippin, translated by Adrian Del Caro, Cambridge University Press, New York.
Nietzsche, F. (1999). *Thus Spake Zarathustra*, translated by Thomas Common, Dover Publications, Inc. Mineola, New York.
Nietzsche, F. (1980). *Thus Spoke Zarathustra*, eds. Giorgio Colli and Mazzino Montinari, Berlin, de Gruyter.
Nietzsche, F. (1967). *Thus Spoke Zarathustra*, translated by R.J. Hollingdale, Penguin Books, Baltimore, Maryland.

Beyond Good and Evil
Nietzsche, F. (2002). *Beyond Good and Evil*, ed. By Rolf-Peter Horstmann and Judith Norman, translated by Judith Norman, Cambridge University Press, New York.
Nietzsche, F. (1989). *Beyond Good and Evil*, translated, with Commentary, by Walter Kaufmann, Vintage Books, A division of Random House, Inc., New York.
Nietzsche, F. (1909). *Beyond Good and Evil*, 136, edited by Dr Oscar Levy, v.5., translated by Helen Zimmern, T.N. Foulis, Edinburgh and London.

A Genealogy of Morals
On The Genealogy of Morals
The Genealogy of Morals
Nietzsche, F. (1989). *On The Genealogy of Morals*, Translated by Walter Kaufmann and R. J. Hollingdale—*Ecce Homo*, Translated by Walter Kaufmann, Edited, with commentary by Walter Kaufmann, Vintage Books, New York.
Nietzsche, F. (1913). *The Genealogy of Morals*, Translated by HORACE B. SAMUEL, M.A., T.N. Foulis, Edinburgh and London.
Nietzsche, F. (1897). *A Genealogy of Morals*, Edited by Alexander Tille, Translated by William A. Hauseman, Poems Translated by John Gray, THE MACMILLAN COMPANY, LONDON.

The Case of Wagner
Nietzsche, F. (1911). *The Case of Wagner ; II. Nietzsche Contra Wagner ; III. Selected Aphorisms*, Translated by Anthony M. Ludovici, (3d ed.), *IV. We Philologists, The Case of Wagner*, Epilogue, Translated by J. M. Kennedy, T. N. Foulis, Edinburgh.

The Twilight of the Idols
   Nietzsche, F. (2007). *The Anti-Christ, Ecce Homo, The Twilight of the Idols, and Other Writing*, Edited by Aaron Ridley and Judith Norman, Translated by Judith Norman, (First published 2005), Cambridge University Press, Cambridge.
   Nietzsche, F. (1899). *The Case of Wagner, Nietzsche contra Wagner, The Twilight of the Idols, The Antichrist.* Translated by Thomas Common, T. Fisher Unwin, London.

The Antichrist/ The Anti-Christ
   Nietzsche, F. (2007). *The Anti-Christ, Ecce Homo, The Twilight of the Idols, and Other Writing*, Edited by Aaron Ridley and Judith Norman, Translated by Judith Norman, (First published 2005), Cambridge University Press, Cambridge.
   Nietzsche, F. (1899). *The Case of Wagner, Nietzsche contra Wagner, The Twilight of the Idols, The Antichrist,* Translated by Thomas Common, T. Fisher Unwin, London

Ecce Homo
   Nietzsche, F. (2007). *Ecce Homo,* Translated with an Introduction and Notes by Duncan Large, Oxford University Press, New York.
   Nietzsche, F. (1989). *Ecce Homo,* Translated by Walter Kaufmann, Edited, with commentary by Walter Kaufmann, Vintage Books, New York.
   Nietzsche, F. (1911). *The Complete Works of Friedrich Nietzsche, Ecce Homo,* Volume Seventeen, Why I Am So Wise, 7, Edited by Dr. Oscar Levy, Translated by Anthony M. Ludovici, Poetry Rendered by: Paul V. Cohen, Herman Scheffauer, Francis Bickley, Dr. G.T. Wrench, The Macmillan Company, New York.

Nietzsche's Last Notebooks 1888/Writing from the Early Notebooks/Writing from the Late Notebooks/Unpublished Writing from the Period of Unfashionable Observations
   Nietzsche, F. (2012). *Nietzsche's Last Notebooks 1888,* Nietzsche's Notebooks in English: a Translator's Introduction and Afterward, Translator Daniel Fidel Ferrer, USA.
   Nietzsche, F. (2010). *Writing from the Early Notebooks,* Edited by Raymond Geuss; Alexander Nehamas, Translated by Ladislaus Löb, (First published 2009), Cambridge University Press, Cambridge.
   Nietzsche, F. (2006). *Writing from the Late Notebooks,* Edited by Rüdiger Bittner, Translated by Kate Strurge, (First published 2003), Cambridge University Press, Cambridge.
   Nietzsche, F. (1995). *The Complete Works of Friedrich Nietzsche,* Volume Eleven, *Unpublished Writing from the Period of Unfashionable Observations,* Translated, with an Afterward, by Richard T. Gray, Stanford University Press, Stanford, California.
   Derrida J. (1979). *Spurs: Nietzsche's Styles, Eperons: les Styles de Nietzsche,* trans. Barbara Harlow University of Chicago Press, Chicago.

Further Reading

a—Books on Nietzsche that reveal other dimensions of what we thought before;
b—Books on Nietzsche explaining and widening his thought;
c—Books that published only aphorisms from books of Nietzsche;
d—Books on aphorisms/quotes/citations/ for philosophers and thinkers;
e—Books as anthology of aphorisms for different philosophers and thinkers;
f—Books full of wisdom.

a—Books on Nietzsche that reveal other dimensions of what we thought before;
a.1. In the *Interpretation of Nietzsche's Second Untimely Meditation* (Martin Heidegger, Indiana University Press, 2016) where Heidegger published seminars on his book on Nietzsche and declares that he is in confrontation with his thought. After decades and after his re-reading him, he changed his mind and he had a positive appropriation for his thought, saying that he is perfectly "understandable", mainly about being, time and the different "kinds" of history (monumental, antiquarian, and critical). He agreed that Nietzsche "knew more than he revealed". Heidegger did not tackle other concepts for Nietzsche such as nihilism, perspectivism, the Ideal, etc.

a.2. Some scholars excluded *Ecce Homo* from Nietzsche's books, because it has been published 19 years after his madness and after 8 years of his death and believing that this "autobiography" book is due to the illness of Nietzsche and should not to be taken seriously. Nicholas D. More demonstrates in his book: *Nietzsche's Last Laugh: Ecce Homo as Satire* (Nicholas D. More, Cambridge University Press, 2014) that Nietzsche was interpreting his philosophy, strategically for him, to survive **his "truths" through irony and satire. The book analyses the form, methodically and structurally, in the different parts of the book, and stipulating that Nietzsche was mocking on philosophy through his life's sufferings! The author contradicted Nietzsche when he wrote, when he was "normal"**, in September of 1886, in a letter to a friend, concerning his book: *Beyond Good and Evil: Prelude to a Philosophy of the Future*: "People will dare read it, I suppose, sometime around the year 2000." (http://www.hamiltonbook.com/Games/the-philosophers-the-100-greatest-thinkers-of-all-time).

b—Books on Nietzsche explaining and widening his thought;
b.1. *Nietzsche, Nihilism and the Philosophy of the Future* (Jeffrey Metzger, Editor, Bloomsbury Academic, 2013).
The book focuses on giving three different interpretations for Nietzsche's Nihilism: first, a self-destructed culture where the "highest values devaluate themselves", therefore the world becomes meaningless; second, when the rational thought can never be compatible with the irrationality (commensurable versus incommensurable); the

third is the combination of the two above, that nihilism is a *sine qua non* of human culture and re-questioning the teleology of the existence itself. Of course, the abundance of the writing on the "nihilism" of Nietzsche and about Nietzsche can be nihilistic too!

b.2. *The Oxford Handbook of Nietzsche* (Ken Gemes, Editor and John Richardson, Editor, Oxford University Press, 2016)

The authors tackle issues on philosophical topics of Nietzsche: Part 1 focuses on biographical questions, Part 2 tackles his relations to other philosophers, while Part 3 discusses his works. Part 4, 5 and 6, explain his notions of "values", "epistemology and metaphysics" and "development of will to power". However, can we truly fantasize that we are explaining Nietzsche and his thoughts? The Interpretations about him are so soulless and tedious!

c—Books that published only aphorisms taken from books of Nietzsche;

The following books are competitors too:

Little Black Classics Aphorisms On Love and Hate (Friedrich Nietzsche, Penguin Little Black Classics, 2015)

And

Nietzsche: Webster's Quotations, Facts and Phrases (Icon Group International, ICON Group International, Inc., 2010)

The first book is a competitor as it includes only aphorisms for Nietzsche about love and hate and the paradoxes that they can create. Love does not contradict hate but they complement each other. To love to hate and to hate to love are essential for existence. This anthology is restricted to two themes only. While the second book is **a compilation of quotations from various sources related to Nietzsche as term. As said this book is a competitor because all readers of Nietzsche will be eager to know what has been said about him in different fields that differ from his own.**

d—Books on aphorisms/quotes/citations/ for philosophers and thinkers;

d.1. *The Bed of Procrustes: Philosophical and Practical Aphorisms* (Nassim Nicholas Taleb, Penguin, 2011)

This book written is in aphorisms, and the main concern is to show the limitations of human knowledge, the way the mind functions and mainly to explain how modernistic society has been transformed, for instance, in changing humans to fit technology; in fudging our ethics to fit our needs for employment. The author explains in his book how his "classical values" make him "advocate the triplet of erudition, elegance, and courage; against modernity's phoniness, nerdiness, and philistinism!" The author is an economist, a lot of his aphorisms concentrate on this field!

d.2. *Peter's Quotations: Ideas for Our Times* (Laurence J. Peter, HarperCollins Publishers, 2013, Collins Reference, 1993, Bantam, 1983, Random House, 1979, William Morrow Co., 1977)

The book is a collection of quotations taken from two multimillion-selling

Laurence J. Peter's books: *The Peter Principle* and *The Peter Prescription*. *Tackling issues about our contemporary problems, addressing for a wide range of categories of people from students to writers, but not to philosophers!*

e—Books as anthology of aphorisms for different philosophers and thinkers;
Concise Oxford Dictionary of Quotations (Susan Ratcliffe, Oxford University Press, 2011)
And
Friendship: A Book of Quotations (Herb Galewitz, Dover Publications, 2012)

The first book (seventh edition, 2012), includes more than 9000 quotations from 2300 philosophers, scientists, scholars, politicians, novelists, writers, poets, song-writers, comedians, actresses, singers, film producers, etc., from different ages, historical and modern ones. Even though the book has a lot of wisdom and diversity of different "levels" of deepness, it is still without one guiding line of thoughts.

The second is similar to the first I mentioned above, however this is on a smaller scale (400 quotations). A compilation, just a compilation!

f—Books full of wisdom.

f.1. *The Black Swan: The Impact of the Highly Improbable* (Nassim Nicholas Taleb, Random House Trade, 2010)

This book advances that the big events in our life are rare, improbable, unpredictable, and randomly occurred, because they are statistically uncertain. The author, under the umbrella of the Systemic Paradigm, is admitting that complex phenomena cannot be explained in a reductionist way (positivism) because we can never be exhaustive. In addition, unknown/hidden causes, human error, risk and decision-making, etc., cannot be predictable. Even though it has been published in 32 languages, has sold close to three million copies and ranks 4372 on Amazon Best Sellers, I can say that two or three aphorisms can encapsulate the entire book!

f.2. *The Alchemist* (Paulo Coelho, HarperOne; 25 Anv. edition 2014)

This is a mystical, fictional book that appears to be giving wisdoms, but in fact is a confidence trickster. While it ranks 2,350 on the Amazon Best Sellers, I found two main wisdoms: the first, "Everyone, when they are young, knows what their Personal Legend is", and the second is, "when you want something, all the universe conspires in helping you to achieve it."

Cune Press

Cune Press was founded in 1994 to publish thoughtful writing of public importance. Our name is derived from "cuneiform." (In Latin *cuni* means "wedge.")

In the ancient Near East the development of cuneiform script—simpler and more adaptable than hieroglyphics—enabled a large class of merchants and landowners to become literate. Clay tablets inscribed with wedge-shaped stylus marks made possible a broad inter-meshing of individual efforts in trade and commerce.

Cuneiform enabled scholarship to exist and art to flower, and created what historians define as the world's first civilization. When the Phoenicians developed their sound-based alphabet, they expressed it in cuneiform.

The idea of Cune Press is the democratization of learning, the faith that rarefied ideas, pulled from dusty pedestals and displayed in the streets, can transform the lives of ordinary people. And it is the conviction that ordinary people, trusted with the most precious gifts of civilization, will give our culture elasticity and depth—a necessity if we are to survive in a time of rapid change.

Aswat: Voices from a Small Planet (a series from Cune Press)

Looking Both Ways	Pauline Kaldas
Stage Warriors	Sarah Imes Borden
Stories My Father Told Me	Helen Zughraib

 Syria Crossroads (a series from Cune Press)

Jinwar & Other Stories	Alex Poppe
Visit the Old City of Aleppo	Khaldoun Fansa
The Dusk Visitor	Musa Al-Halool
Steel & Silk	Sami Moubayed
The Passionate Spies	John Harte
The Road from Damascus	Scott C. Davis
A Pen of Damascus Steel	Ali Ferzat
White Carnations	Musa Rahum Abbas

 Bridge Between the Cultures (a series from Cune Press)

Confessions of a Knight Errant	Gretchen McCullough
Afghanistan & Beyond	Linda Sartor
Apartheid is a Crime	Mats Svensson
Arab Boy Delivered	Paul Aziz Zarou
Congo Prophet	Frederic Hunter
Music Has No Boundaries	Rafique Gangat

Cune Cune Press: www.cunepress.com

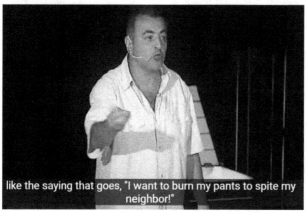

like the saying that goes, "I want to burn my pants to spite my neighbor!"

Farid Younes TEDxBeirut

FARID YOUNES COMBINES TWO OPPOSITES: He is devoted to serious ideas . . . and yet he pursues them with the glee and abandon of a boy at his birthday party. He is a beloved teacher, because he designs buildings and cities . . . so his rarefied ideas *do* have a tangible outlet.

It is hard to overestimate the appeal of a kind man who is devoted to thinking and craftsmanship . . . in a land where insane violence and governmental incompetence have made a frontal assault on Lebanese culture—which is probably the finest and most appealing way of thinking, living, and being . . . ever.

Farid has served as the Chair of Architecture at Notre Dame University, Lebanon with a PhD from U of Montreal in Canada. When he is not sipping wine at the stunning Calatrava Winery or munching tasty morsels at the Darien Restaurant, Farid enjoys chit-chatting about Sacred Art and Architecture, the intersection of Maronite Christianity and Islam, and the intertwining of Sociology in Architecture. A favorite subject is the musico - architectural theory of the Pythagoro - Platonic. Be sure to ask him about his concept of "Resonant Architecture" . . . specifically the way Architecture and Music reflected each other during the Abbasid phase of the great medieval Islamic Empire.

Farid also has fun with City Streets. He never misses a meeting of the City Street Technical Committee at his university.

Naturally, a guy with this much delight in virtually everything a person can do with his or her mind is in mad demand as a judge for competitions in his field. If you think that students must follow this man through the streets, well, you would be right about that.

In a world where brutish ardor seems to be the order of the day, Farid Younes is one who loves to think and to build. You gotta love this man!

—Scott C. Davis

CPSIA information can be obtained
at www.ICGtesting.com
Printed in the USA
JSHW030513170422
24885JS00013B/14

9 781951 082017